THE

Pleasures of Cruelty;

BEING

a sequel to the reading of

JUSTINE ET JULIETTE

BY

THE MARQUIS DE SADE

———

CONSTANTINOPLE, PARIS
ET LONDON

———

BIRCHGROVE PRESS

Copyright © 2011 Birchgrove Press
All rights reserved.

http://www.birchgrovepress.com

ISBN:
978-0-9870956-2-6

An extract from *The Pleasures of Cruelty*, entitled 'The Sultan's Reverie,' was published in *The Pearl: A Journal of Facetiæ and Voluptuous Reading* in December 1880 (Number 18), which was published by William Lazenby. The first complete edition (three volumes in one) appears to have been published in 1886, possibly by Lazenby, with a false but, in the context of the story that it elaborates, appropriate place of publication: Constantinople. An edition was also published in 'Paris et London' in 1898, probably by Leonard Smithers and Duringe. The author is unknown. Peter Mendes suggests that it was most probably written by one or more members of the flagellant and erotica writing coterie that gathered around Richard Monckton-Milnes, possible author of *The Rodiad* and owner of one of the finest collections of erotica in Victorian England. See Peter Mendes, *Clandestine Erotic Fiction in English 1800-1930: A Bibliographical Study*. (Aldershot: Scolar Press, 1993; p. 156) Colonel, later General, John Studholme Hodgson, a member of Milnes' circle, is an excellent authorial candidate. According to Milnes, Sir Richard Burton noted Studholme Hodgson's penchant for cruelty, and Studholme Hodgson's involvement in the writing of an earlier work focusing on the pleasures of flogging, *Revelries! and Devilries!! or Scenes in the Life of Sir Lionel Heythorp* (William Dugdale, 1867), has been suggested.

CONTENTS

THE

Pleasures of Cruelty

INTRODUCTION

Sir Charles Dacre (a wealthy baronet, one of the boon companions of George IV) at the early age of thirty-eight finds himself the mere wreck a man, a used-up sensualist, whose youthful vigour has been spent and wasted in debauchery. Left a widower with three lovely daughters, Maud, Alice and Flora, aged respectively eighteen, fifteen and seventeen, he yet finds the depression of his spirits so great as to compel him to seek every possible amusement in gambling or debauchery to be found in Brussels, Vienna or Paris, leaving his girls entirely to the care of their governess, although they all travelled in company from place to place.

Nothing gives him pleasure. The most erotic devices fail to excite his morbid sensibility, in fact, he one day expressed himself to Madame Josephine, a noted procuress (in whose house he happened to be), as utterly incapable of experiencing sensual pleasure.

The lady offered to rejuvenate him for a fee of five hundred pounds. The agreement was made, but Madam told him it was by means of his three beautiful young daughters that her ideas were to be carried out, and that he would find inflicting outrage, shame and humiliation on them would have such an effect as it was not possible for him to imagine.

Such delicately and modestly brought up girls would revolt at the scenes to which he would introduce and compel them to take part in; that they should be whipped, tortured and debased in every possible manner, whilst he would find himself stimulated by the idea of outraging his own flesh and blood, yielding only to fearful compulsion, so different to the voluntary submission to be purchased by money.

"Can you steel your heart so as to do all this! If so, you must secure a residence in some country where the language is strange and barbarous—say Bulgaria, Servia or, better still, on the Asiatic side of the Bosphorus—.

"The Turks would never dream of interfering; the girls should be kept veiled and pass as your wives; you, yourself, an Englishman fond of Turkey, and adopting their customs; however, they might rebel, they must submit to the means we could use, without slightest fear.

"If you agree to my proposal, you must engage me to accompany you, and take my maid Augustine (who is used to such things) for servant. Fit one room up as a torture chamber, with double windows, and padded all round as to prevent all noises from reaching the outside; fitted up with a post and a ladder against the wall, for tying up, and whips and scourges of all sorts. We could also, if necessary, use bunches of holly, and stinging nettles; but my best idea is to reside somewhere near the Lake of Apollonia, a beautiful but very solitary and secluded spot, not far from the sea of Marmora, where you will find first rate shooting and fishing to divert yourself with, and vary your amusement, and also, I am informed a famous spot for the growth of prickly teazles, such as they use in the preparation of velvets, and more valuable for our purpose."

All this, and much more, so fired the imagination of Sir Charles, that he readily assented to make the experiment, and all the necessary arrangements being carried out as speedily as possible, Madame Josephine assuming the role of governess (the old one being dispensed with.)

The writer omits unnecessary preliminaries and assumes them to be comfortably settled in their new house, which it is needless to describe.

Part the First

The Torture Chamber

Sir Charles does not long delay to make practical proof of the experiments. The very first evening everything can be in readiness he arranges with Madame to begin with Flora and Alice, who are ordered to attend him in the padded room within fifteen minutes. Then he ascends to the chamber where Madame awaits him, and taking a glass of wine herself, offers one to him, asking if he is quite sure he is prepared to go through the experiment to the uttermost.

Sir Charles: "The sooner, the better; you will find me as relentless as you could wish."

Madam: "They will shriek and appeal to your fatherly love for protection."

Sir Charles: "I will laugh at their shamefaced distress and horrify them still more."

Madam: "Suppose they scream too loudly?"

Sir Charles: "It will only make me more excited; neither tears fainting, or blood, will move me from my purpose."

Madam: "Suppose they hide their faces in disgust?"

Sir Charles: "I will kick them and tie their hands behind their backs, so they must see my excited prick: they shall take it in their hands and kiss it till the spunk flies in their faces."

Madam: "Ah! Ah! you quite enter into it as you ought; you must watch every minutiae and take pleasure in their contortions, writhings and looks of horror and disgust, their tears and blushes, the agonized expression of pain, also the contractions of the muscles of the young ladies' legs, thighs and bottoms, the glowing tints and trickling blood as the rod is well applied."

Sir Charles: "Damme! you seem going to start the whipping pretty hard at first."

Madam: "Can you stand the sight of your own daughters, cruelly and shamefully whipped; it is a glorious sight."

Sir Charles: "Above all things, it must be delicious; whilst you flog them I shall insult them, kiss their cunnies, or frig them with my fingers."

Madam: "I thought so; you'll soon want to whip them yourself; you must have been a cruel sensual man in your time and many a little virgin cunny has been, doubtless, outraged and torn by your tremendous cock; what a fascinating fancy it is to men to have in their power poor helpless little girls, whose small unfledged affairs are scarcely big enough for a boy to enter, and the forcing of which is a most savage delight to the sensualists. I, too, love to have them young. Give me a beautiful young girl a lady by birth and training, delicately, modestly, and if possible, religiously brought up (it adds to her repulsive, horrified ideas), stripped to her drawers, her face scarlet with shame, wincing and shrinking over the first few skilfully administered strokes, lightly given with insulting expressions and derisive laughter, then screaming and yelling with pain, as you proceed to thrash her earnestly, making her leap about 'til her drawers hang in tatters, stopping every few strokes to give her quivering bottom a hearty spank with your open hand, put your finger up her bottom to disgust her, watch the blood trickling down her pretty legs; then make her put on another pair of drawers, which open only in front, fix her in a stooping position, so as to bring them tight across her bottom, and with a few skilful strokes and cruel, chaffing remarks, cut them open for her like a proper pair, telling her she can now ease herself properly and you hope her bum is not too sore to be wiped."

Sir Charles: "But surely no girl could stand all that, she must faint?" (the idea is so exciting his priapus is almost ready to burst out of his breeches).

Madam: "Of course she would; I have spent many a time making a girl faint under the rod. I like to hear the screams getting fainter and fainter, as they are going off; then, just as she's going off, tear out one or two of the little hairs from her slit; this gives such exquisite agony as always to revive them for a time, but the finger frigging, especially in their bottoms, is the most exciting, as they are in such a state of warmth and lubricity it is impossible for them to contain themselves however disgusting it may seem; then go on again with birch till you finally finish her off. If in my place, you can lay her unconscious form on a bed or sofa, contemplate the pulsating and blushing rosy grotto of pleasure, and finally open the poor lacerated thighs and plunge into her heated cunny, and work away till you experience the delight of her revival under your invigorating strokes, feel her bottom gradually respond to your thrusts, writhe and twist with the delicious sensations you have inspired her with, the rapturous spendings mixed with your own, and after all her expression of shame and humiliation as she comprehends it all, and how she has given way to her feelings, then is the time for another touch of the rod with insulting and obscene reflections as to how she enjoyed it."

Here Madame breaks off to laugh at Sir Charles, who mad with excitement, has taken out his concern and is frigging himself; but a knock at the door causes him to button up hastily and they both look as grave as possible when Flora and Alice enter.

Madame, as she locks the door: "You've not hurried yourselves, young ladies?"

Then she whispers to Sir Charles that she is going to commence by showing him what excitement is to be got by watching a modest girl's confusion.

"Flora and Alice," says she, turning to them, and speaking sternly, "your papa wishes to see which of you has the best legs and figure."

They start, blush and stammer out.

"No, no, Madame Josephine, we can't do that, it is so indelicate, Papa can never have thought of such a thing!"

Taking no notice of their answer, she calmly orders them to stand in the middle of the room and raise their petticoats to their knees.

"Oh, Sir Charles dear father don't let that woman insult us so, it's most indecent; do, papa, protect us. They cling to him and Alice kisses and begs of him with tears in her eyes. He takes his cigar from his mouth and rudely repulses her with a puff of smoke in her face and laughing says:

"Whatever your governess orders must be for your good."

This unexpected and mortifying rebuff only added to their agitation.

Pale and frightened, Flora throws herself on an ottoman, burying her face in her hands, whilst the terrified little Alice runs to the door sobbing as if her heart would break but there is neither pity nor exit for them.

Madame calmly repeats her order; then taking up a light lady's riding whip steps across the room and gives Flora a slight cut across her hands. The poor girl, in her agony, shrieks and clasps her hands, but received two additional cuts across each cheek, plainly leaving their mark on the previously crimsoned face.

"Oh! Oh!" she screams at each cut, "Papa, Papa, have mercy," but Madame with great quickness, gave another hard cut, which also left a deep red mark across the poor girl's neck.

"Will you, you obstinate girl," said she calmly, "obey your father's wishes?"

The victim darts behind Sir Charles' chair, hoping that would protect her, but Madame follows up with the little whip.

"Swish—swish—swish" cut across arms, face, or neck, leaving their tell-tale marks.

Flora screamed piteously "Ah-r-r-re. Ah-r-r-re! Mercy Madame. Mercy dear father. I shall be cut to pieces. Oh! I will—I will—I will, indeed!"

Flora's face is bleeding, and her tearful eyes express both terror and humiliation; but, without a pause, Madame turns to Alice, raising the whip.

"Do you want this, too; or will you submit. See what your sister's obstinacy has done for her. I'll teach you both to obey instantly whatever you are ordered to do," she said.

Alice is a timid, fragile thing, with a most spiritual expression, so different from the determination of her sister whose pitiable plight has such a terrible effect on the timid girl that she instantly pleads for mercy.

"Oh! Oh! I will do anything!" she screams, "if you don't hit me, dear Madame."

Madame quietly resumes her seat, and then orders them to place themselves in front of their papa, facing him, and then to raise their clothes to their knees.

"Look your papa straight in the face, or I will let your delicate bottoms feel my whip."

The poor girls, sobbing, blushing, and not daring even to droop their eyelids, nervously clutch their petticoats, and raise them to the required height, Madame remarking about to Sir Charles:

"They little know what I will make them do yet—much as they feel insulted and degraded by this."

The poor girls moan and sigh.

Sir Charles, feeling the sensual excitement, exclaims:

"Look straight at me, don't close your eyes; mind how you hold your clothes!"

Madame: "Pull them up higher. Alice, your flannel petticoat is not quite up. Sir Charles wants to see your drawers properly."

Flora's drawers, of the finest white linen, are beautifully embroidered with open needlework, whilst Alice has only a nice trimming of Brussels lace on hers; the effect is most charming; the blushing faces and agitated features contrast so strangely with the quiet loveliness of their sweet legs, encased in pink silk stockings, blue garters and gold buckles, just above the knees, and slightly concealed by the drawers, and lower down the eyes feast on the delicately-heeled shoes of dove coloured satin. Madame makes Sir Charles feel their legs and pass his hands over their beautiful calves, calls his attention to her refined taste, in the drawers she had provided for his daughters, and then orders them to turn around and lift their clothes to give a back view.

"Draw up the legs of your drawers my dears," she says so as to let Papa see a little of the beautiful white flesh of your thighs. Do you hear what I say? Make haste or you'll both catch it smartly"; at the same time giving a smart little whisk of the whip so as just to touch Alice on the bare part above her garters eliciting a slight scream from the girl who expected some more to follow.

For more than a quarter of an hour Sir Charles and Madame handle their legs and feel the bare thighs, so soft, velvety and firm, comparing Alice's slender make with the more sturdy figure of Flora; the she-devil of a Frenchwoman even passing her hand up their drawers, telling Sir Charles that one was nicely fledged, whilst the little one had scarcely yet begun to grow her maiden moustache.

The two girls are more confused than ever, but Madame, without giving them time for recovery or reflection, says it is time to go a little further, and tells Flora she fears she is as obstinate as ever, and must be yet more degraded and humiliated, ordering her to pull up her petticoats to her waist.

The poor girl, bursting into hysterical crying, falls on her knees, begging and praying her father to spare her:

"Oh! Father! Father! spare me; how can you love me and let that woman treat us so?"

Sir Charles in a passion, gives her a sound box on the ears, exclaiming: "You hussey, do as you are bid, this minute; Madame Josephine will know how to make you respect her."

"Indeed, she will," says Madame, "take that, and that, and that," slashing away with assumed rage, across the shoulders of the kneeling girl, each blow leaving its red mark, where it touched her delicate neck. "You will have to mind that woman's orders or every part of your body will smart for it."

Choking, sobbing and ready to faint with fear and pain, she springs to her feet, shrieking for mercy. "Oh! Oh! Oh! Madame, say what you want, I will do anything!"

Madame: "Face me, with your back to your Papa, raise your clothes!"

Flora: "There, Madame, will that do?" pulling everything up to her hips, so as to show the beautiful contour of her posteriors, in her well-filled drawers, which are slightly gaping open behind, so as to give Sir Charles a little glimpse of her bottom, where the chemise has got tucked up.

Madame: "Higher, up higher," cutting with the whip round her buttocks so as just to catch the exposed flesh behind, leaving a beautiful mark for Sir Charles to contemplate.

Flora: "Ah-r-r-re! Oh! Do have pity," raising her clothes as high as possible under her arms.

Madame: "Now, say your catechism, word for word, after me;" flourishing the dreadful little whip—"shall I open my drawers, Papa?"

Flora: "Oh! that will show—my—my—behind."

Madame giving another cut: "It's not your business what you show but to repeat my words."

Flora: "Ah! Ah! Madame pity! Papa do you want to see my drawers open?"

Sir Charles: "Answer properly Miss Pert—no questions!"

Madame: "May I show you my bare bottom, Papa?"

Flora: "May I show you my bare bottom Papa?" She is crimson to the roots of her hair. Sir Charles and Madame laugh immoderately at her confusion.

Madame: "Now, Flora, open your drawers behind and ask your Papa if it pleases him to see your bottom."

Flora: "Papa, Papa, is it your pleasure?" Her tongue seems almost unable to utter the words, but she stammers out: "Does it really please you?" Her sobs and shame quite overcome her.

Madame: "Miss, speak out! no shamefacedness will

avail you. Ask Papa if you shall pull open your bottom for him to see; speak up, you squeamish little fool; quick, quick;" giving two more cuts so the end of the whip reaches her exposed bottom again.

Poor Flora quickly complies, she is so cowed and distressed.

Madame: "'Keep in that position at your peril. Now Alice, your turn will come, unless you implicitly obey my orders, you shall be whipped till the skin comes off, if I have to take you in hand."

Alice: "Oh! Dear Madame, anything rather than that, and to please Papa."

Madame: "You must slap Flora's bottom twenty-four times, with your open hand, and do it hard."

The poor girl, bewildered and confused, casts her tearful eyes towards Sir Charles, but meets no sympathy there; his face only expresses a sardonic satisfaction as Flora appeals to her sister for pity: "Alice dear, you surely won't help to torture me?"

Alice, bathed in tears, assures her it is only under compulsion and to save them both from cruel whippings.

Madame: "Now, girls, this sentimental nonsense is useless; how often must I keep saying that, and giving cuts of my whip to enforce obedience; begin at once or your own bottom will pay for the delay, without saving your sister. Begin! Begin! Begin!" each word bringing a sharp cut on Alice's reluctant hands.

"Kiss Flora's bottom first you little minx."

Alice: "Flora dear, do forgive me;" giving the required kiss with a loving earnestness; "if it was only that I would kiss you all over."

Madame, with another cut: "Are you going to begin; we'll see about that bye and bye."

Alice: "Yes, yes, Madame," spanking poor Flora's bottom rapidly, but not very hard.

Madame: "Harder, harder;" counting each slap, "not so fast, let her feel each one properly," waving the whip in a threatening manner.

Flora, writhing at each slap: "Ah! Ah! Oh! Alice, my bottom's so sore, do pity me, if the others wont."

Alice is in tears, and crimson with shame, as each slap is distinctly heard, and seem to bring a rosy flush on the exposed cheeks of her sister's bottom; she exclaimed: "Dear Flora, forgive me, as I will you if you are compelled to strike me."

Madame to Flora: "Mind you keep your drawers well open, you slut, or it will be still worse."

The victim bites her lips in agony; till the blood comes, and strives hard to obey the cruel orders.

At last as the twenty-fourth slap is given, Sir Charles is so excited that he exposes his concern, to his horrified daughters, and wants to spend over the smarting bottom, but Madame Josephine promptly gives his burning and palpitating pego a switch with her whip, as she orders him to do it in her face, as so much more humiliating and disgusting to a sensitive girl; Flora is made to kneel down, and in that position, receives a tremendous discharge of sperm all over her face. They laugh at the sight of it running down her cheeks, and Madame, to add to her confusion, and still more to excite Sir Charles by the sight of the horrified and disgusting looks of his daughter, makes her wipe some of it into her mouth.

Sir Charles' sensations of voluptuous enjoyment are of the keenest description and he exclaims, as he sinks back in his chair:

"Ah! Ah! Madame you are indeed a witch, to bring me back to such experiences as I have not had for years."

Flora is still on her knees, with her face buried in her hands, when Madame orders Alice to raise her sister's clothes behind and open her drawers, so as again to expose the still smarting and blushing bottom, which she gives a smart cut with her whip, raising a long red weal, and orders Flora to widen out her legs and remain as she is. "Now Alice," says she, "put your finger up her bottom and work it up and down."

"Oh! Oh! Ah! Ah-r-r-re! You're hurting me; oh it hurts so, it can't go in," screams Flora.

Alice: "I won't do it dear; they shall cut me to pieces first!"

Madame: "How dare you say that? Turn up your clothes and open your own drawers, Miss, how do you like that, and that," raising great smarting weals on poor Alice's bottom at each cut, "how do you like that; are you going to be obstinate, like your sister?"

Alice: Shrieking with the intense pain: "Mercy! Oh! Mercy! I will, I must do it, or I shall die!"

Madame: "Then, wet your finger in your mouth; that's right; do it again and again; after each insertion it will go further in;" laughing at the poor girl's disgust, as well as shame and indignation, as she sodomizes her sister with her finger.

Poor Flora in spite of her indignation at this fresh insult cannot help wriggling and writhing her bottom, as her sister's motions have a soothing effect upon the burning warmth of the parts, which causes Sir Charles great amusement, and as a finish off, the victim is ordered to put Alice's finger in her mouth and suck it clean.

Madame: "Sir Charles, shall I tell you a good story about a French gentleman I knew, who, having been refused on account of his age, by a young German lady of eighteen, resolved in revenge, to watch his opportunity of catching her alone, and compelling her to follow him to some unfrequented spot, where she could be completely in his power.

Sir Charles: "Go on, I should like to hear it."

Madame: "Then to begin, the Lady Emmeline was only daughter and sole heiress to the baron Kuntze who owned and generally resided upon a vast patrimonial estate, near the borders of Switzerland, in the Black Forest; the gentleman, Monsieur de Longuevitte, was a scion of one of the noblest families in France, a man of middle age, and fine prepossessing appearance, but unfortunately only too well known for his previous looseness of life, gambling and extravagance, who was anxious to recover his reduced fortunes by securing the Baron's wealthy daughter, independently of which, her deep blue eyes, golden hair, and lovely healthy beauty, had quite impressed the Parisien roué, when he first encountered her by chance, in one of his economical tours, which he had to take from time to time, to allow his income to meet his liabilities.

Unfortunately for him, the lady heard such unfavourable accounts of his usual manner of life, that she was blind to all his fascinations, and flatly refused to even consider his addresses, as she stated he was much to old for her.

Monsieur, not only wounded at heart, but hurt in his vanity, disappeared, secretly vowing revenge; for some months, he returned to his old pursuits and took advice from myself and others, how both to have a deep revenge as well as cruelly compel Mademoiselle Emmeline to become his wife unconditionally.

Having settled a plan of operations which seemed like to succeed, he proceeded to the neighbourhood, disguised as a Swiss peasant and having well reconnoitred the place he bribed a priest to be ready to marry him at any time to a lady he intended to elope with, as soon as it could be managed.

About a mile from the old Baron's modernized castle ran a clear sparkling stream well stocked with trout crossed at one spot by a bridge of stone affording the only possible communication with the nearest village. Emmeline, being a fine horsewoman, frequently passed that way on her beautiful grey steed, with an English retriever as her sole attendant.

M. de Longuevitte, so disguised that even his own mother would not have known him stationed himself at this point, apparently engaged in fishing, which, although conducted by him on anything but scientific principles, was very successful in such a sequestered spot, where the finny tribe were seldom interfered with. On the third day he heard some one approaching on horseback, and displaying his piscatorial trophies on the green-sward, was delighted to see the un-suspecting Emmeline cantering towards the bridge.

"You seem to have had good success, my man," said she, reining in her steed, "will you sell your fish, my father is so fond of trout, but no one ever troubles to catch them."

"Willingly, my lady," said the disguised fisherman, "but how will you take them?"

"I'm only going to the village, and shall be back in little more than an hour," said she. "I will get a little basket there and then take my father an agreeable surprise."

"Very well, my lady, if I am not exactly as this spot, you will find me a little further up the stream; there is a favourite place of mine behind those trees," said the peasant, pointing to a clump of trees about a quarter of a mile distant.

"That will do," exclaimed Emmeline Kuntze, as she galloped off, little thinking of what was to happen. Of course, before she returned, Monsieur took care to remove to the spot indicated; the bridge was quite lonely enough for his purpose, but the clump of trees was better still, and his heart leaped with excitement as he caught a glimpse of her returning, and looking for him alone the banks of the stream.

"I should like to see you catch two or three." said she, pulling up; "so I made haste back half an hour before my time; if I only knew how I might catch them myself another time."

"Allow me, my lady, to tie up your horse," said the peasant, assisting her to dismount.

As soon as her feet touch the ground, "now, my pretty lady, you are in my power; attempt to escape and I will shoot you dead", said he presenting a loaded pistol to her breast.

"Mercy! Mercy!" cries the affrightened Emmeline, "don't murder me, what shall I give you? I have not much money, take my watch, my diamond ring, anything, but spare my life."

"See how I will serve you," says the peasant, shooting the retriever dead at her side. "Come a little further up the stream with me that I may examine what you have got; do exactly as I order you or the other barrel will drive a bullet through your heart."

Taking the bridle of the horse in one hand and the pistol in the other he compels her to keep slightly in front of him till they have advanced a considerable distance into a wild thicket; he halts at the foot of a little cascade just as the horse raises his tail and evacuates some rather loose excrement.

"The very thing I want," exclaimed the peasant, "now, Mademoiselle, take off your drawers, or I'll fire; no one can help you, you don't leave this spot alive, unless you do everything I order, come, quick, off with them."

She obeys with frightened, blushing confusion.

"You need not be so particular about keeping your

dress, so as to hide yourself, we'll see what you are like presently."

Peasant: "Now, lady Emmeline you see I know who you are, just rub your drawers into that soft horse dung; you'll find it nice," said he, smearing a piece on her face.

Victim: "You dirty, cruel man!"

Peasant: "Obey, or I fire; no objections, it's my pleasure, and you must do it if you wish to live; now do it well."

Victim: "It's horrible, disgusting," as she slowly executes his order.

Peasant, producing a small knife, and some tape: "Now, cut me a fine bunch of those twigs of willow, strip the leaves off, and tie it up into a handy switch, hold here, just put these two pieces of prickly teazle in the centre; ah! Ha! that will do; hand it to me."

She is now ordered to kneel down, and raise her clothes behind, so as fully to expose her bare bottom.

Peasant: "Keep those drawers on the ground in front of you, pull your chemise up higher; there, there, keep so, or I'll kill you; how do you like that?" Swish—swish—swishing with the rod of twigs each blow leaving deep red marks, and suffusing the whole surface with a rosy blush.

"Ha! Ha! how do you like that proud young lady? Now just lick all that muck off your drawers as quickly as possible."

Victim: "Oh! Oh! I can't, it's so disgusting; it's too dreadful. Ah-r-r-re!" she shrieks as he gives a tremendous whack, and she feels the prickly teazles tearing her tender skin.

Peasant: "Lick it up, lick it up, my dear. Ha! Ha! I know it's beautiful; make haste!" whipping away with great energy.

Victim: "Mercy! Mercy! I'll promise anything; oh!

You'll kill me; I'm full of thorns! Oh! dear! Don't," she shrieks again.

Peasant: "Go on, go on," cutting harder than ever with the rod, till at last her posteriors are torn, mangled and bleeding all over. "Will you, will you marry me?" he exclaims, giving his blows so as to cut between the tender surfaces of the upper parts of her thighs; "does that sting, eh? I thought so! how did you like that last little swish?"

The victim is groaning and ready to faint with agony and shame as he places himself in front of her, with his great, angry looking, red-headed priapus in his left hand, actually touching her nose.

"Now, look up at me," he exclaims, "I want to see how pretty you look, and how pleased you are at my offer of marriage; you don't leave here except for your grave, unless you swear by all that's holy to marry me immediately, and remember the loaded pistol will be close by till you are my wife; what do you say? how pleased you look to get such a nice fellow as I am, my lovely Emmeline!"

Poor Emmeline, more dead than alive shows all the contortions of indignation and disgust in her countenance the marks of her tears across the heated red, smeared face, as her horrified eyes behold the terrible weapon, which virgin as she is, she knows too well will complete her ruin; gasping and sobbing. "Spare me, spare me! Oh! save my life! Oh! how I have suffered!"

Peasant: "Now open your mouth wide and look at me; I'm to be your husband, remember, so I must make you obedient!" Saying which, he can contain himself no longer, but spouts out a deluge of spendings over her face and down her throat.

"Now," says he, "put on your beautiful clean drawers and get home. I hope your bottom won't be too sore to ride; but you haven't far to go; my friend the priest will soon make us man and wife; draw back at your peril if you wish to live; I am de Longuevitte."

Judge her surprise and indignation but reflecting on his desperate character and the impossibility of revealing the outrages she has had to suffer, she made no resistance and within an hour she promised to love, honour and obey, in the most orthodox manner; "and," said he, "by Jove, I think you will after the lesson you have had; talk of 'Taming the Shrew!' why Petruchio was not half up to his business to take so much trouble as he did with Katherine."

Sir Charles: "Ha! Ha! It's the best story I ever heard. I hope you paid attention girls!" turning to his sobbing and crying daughters.

Madame: "I hope so too, for we are now going to progress a little further. Young ladies strip, strip stark naked is the order;" giving each one of them a quick slash or two to make them look sharp.

"Ah! How cruel!" screams Alice, as she and Flora hasten to throw off their dresses. "Oh! dear papa, spare us such complete humiliation!"

He laughs and attempts to kick the poor girl, who fortunately avoids the brutal foot.

Madame interrupting: "Stay; not quite so fast. I always like to look at a girl, with her flannel petticoats just allowing the ends of her drawers to be seen below them. How pretty they look now."

Sir Charles: "See their heaving bosoms, what graceful motions;" making them skip with pain, by sharp cuts on the calves of their legs. "Alice, my dear, say to your Papa, that you trust he is enjoying the fun of seeing his daughters undressing."

Alice, quaking with fear, can scarcely articulate, and commences in a low key, not much above a whisper: "Papa, Papa, I hope you enjoy."

Madame, with a threatening flourish of the whip, instantly persuades her to speak out: "Papa, I hope you enjoy our undressing before you?"

Sir Charles laughs heartily at his daughter's confusion. "'Oh! yes, Alice," he replies, "but to tell you the truth. I am longing to see you both stark naked before me; ah! you may well blush, but I can't, it's so delicious; my love for you both makes the pleasure more exquisite."

Madame: "Now, young ladies, off with your flannel petticoats, drawers and chemises. There's a pretty sight!" she continued, turning to Sir Charles, and pointing at the two girls, as with streaming eyes and confused terrified faces, they stood up to slip off their drawers. "Now, my dears, take them off slowly, so we may observe every motion of your bodies; mind you don't expose your persons too much; it's so indelicate. Why Flora, you are letting us see what's at the bottom of your belly; shameful, Miss, to expose yourself so; giving a cut at the part indicated.

"Now, unlace your stays. Sir Charles have you noticed the elegance of those blue silk corsets and crimson laces, how they set off the figure, but all must come off, after all nature is the prettiest, as we shall soon see."

"Now girls, off with that last rag!" as they now hide their blushing cunnies.

"Ah! you won't!" as they hesitate. "Why, then, don't you make haste?" making Flora scream, as she cuts with the whip across her bare shoulders.

"Now Alice, you're both alike;" giving her a nice little swish across her bottom which has nothing but the chemise to protect it.

Alice: "Oh! Ah! Ah-r-r-re! Mercy! you told us to be slow, and then whip us all the same."

Madame: "No impertinence, Miss, mind what I order;

stand up side by side so we can see the difference between you. Hands off! stand straight!" cutting with the whip to prevent their endeavours to hide their blushing cunnies.

"Look, Sir Charles, see how nicely Flora's mount is covered with almost golden down, but there's nothing to notice on Alice," touching each slightly with the whip on the part indicated.

Sir Charles handles and feels them all over, kneeling down and kissing both their virgin slits which he slightly opens with his finger, plucking the little hairs with fiendish delight. As they scream for mercy, Madame keeps them in continual agitation with her little "swish tail," whip, and at last their agony and confusion quite overcome all other thoughts or fears, as they fall on their knees, begging their obdurate parent to have pity. But he slaps their faces, and Madame gives such sharp reminders, exclaiming: "Now, do exactly as I tell you; you are on your knees, lean forward, and with your hands open the cheeks of your bottoms, so as to show all that is there; keep your heads down;" giving Flora a cut over her head. "Now Alice, hold your bottom well open;" giving a frightful cut across the loins leaving a long red weal and eliciting fearful screams of pain from the poor girl, then as a finish to the tableau, slightly touches each bottom hole with a whisk of the whip.

Alice is now made to kneel exactly behind Flora, and renew the bottom frigging with her finger, whilst Sir Charles, with his breeches down, kneels in front of his eldest girl, who is compelled to do the same to him.

Madame superintends the proper execution of this exercise, cutting the girls with her whip to make them wet their fingers in their mouths, so as to work easily.

"Now, Sir Charles," she exclaims, "you are also one of my pupils;" giving him several cuts which leave their tell-tale marks on his dark-skinned, tough-looking posteriors. This goes on for several minutes till she perceives it cannot be carried on much longer, without bringing him to a climax.

Madame: "Hold! Hold! Enough of that; now, I will show you my style of enjoyment," making Flora put her hands behind her back and handcuffing them.

"Now, Sir Charles, do you take Alice across your knee, whilst you see me amuse myself with Flora."

The excited and lustful parent, who has kicked off his trousers to be at freedom, catches hold of Alice, and lays her across his knee, making her, by a tremendous cut on her bottom, obey his orders, to take hold of his pego, feel how hard and hairy it is, and play with it; he frigs her bottom with his fingers, every now and then making her scream again by a sudden slap on her naked buttocks, Madame having secured her victim to the whipping post by her hands, makes the poor girl stretch her legs wide, and secures her ankles to rings in the floor, nearly two feet apart, then taking a kind of rod formed of a bunch of stinging nettles fixed on a wooden handle, touches Flora all over her belly with them.

Flora, (in terror): "Ah! Ah! Oh! Madame spare me!"

Madame: "It's only the beginning; open your legs well, ah! ha! I needn't order that; you can't help yourself, they are kept open for you, my dear."

Flora: Instinctively struggling to close her thighs, causes herself great pain, especially to her wrists and arms. "Oh! Ah! I shall die if you do it!"

Madame (dashing the nettles into her face): "Kiss them; call to your father, my dear, he's such a nice kind gentleman, couldn't kill a fly for himself, he's so tender hearted."

Flora: "Oh! Oh! Dear father, do pity me;" she sobs hysterically, "don't shame me so!"

Sir Charles: "Your legs are not open wide enough; look, look, Alice," he laughs, "see how Flora enjoys it, but she's rather shamefaced."

Madame (touching and rubbing her mount with the nettles): "How, how do you like that?" and as Flora tries to shut her legs; "well see if it's better behind," thrashing her poor bruised and lacerated bottom.

Flora: "Oh! Oh! My God! Have mercy, spare me from such a fiend!" shrieking with agony.

Madame: "Ah! Now the pretty lips of your pussey are nicely stretched," holding them open with one hand; "look, look, Sir Charles," she exclaims, as she thrusts the fearful bunch of nettles almost into the vagina of the poor victim, who writhes and screams in the most acute agony.

"Pretending to faint are you?" seeing the prostrate state of the poor girl, "but this will revive you," stinging her all over her face, neck and breasts, also especially just under her nose, which prevents her going off.

The nettles are now thrown aside, and her hands unfastened. Madame then orders her to resume her drawers, telling Sir Charles she is going to thrash the girl with her drawers on.

"Now, Miss," she says, "you shall see how clever I am in cutting open drawers which have no proper slit behind; come to the ladder, that is the proper thing to stretch you on."

Flora: "Oh! Father! Help! Madame have mercy," cries she, as she is dragged across the room.

Madame: "Your screams are like music, what do you think, Sir Charles?"

Flora: "Oh! Kill me! Put me out of my misery; father, have you no pity?"

Madame, with the assistance of Sir Charles, secures her still handcuffed hands above her head to one of the steps of the ladder, saying, "you may have the use of your legs to caper about; your drawers (coolly examining them) are beautifully fine, but still very strong, and it will take some thrashing to cut them open; so much the worse for you, Flora, I'm afraid."

Madame feels all about the poor girl's bottom, pinching the bruised flesh; makes her lift up one leg, then the other, as she feels and fiendishly pinches the lips of her cunny, the little clitoris and the lacerated parts of her inner thighs.

Flora (screaming): "Papa, Papa, save me! Oh! Oh! Help! You couldn't be so cruel; you're surely not going to murder me?"

Sir Charles: "That's right Flora, we like to hear you give tongue; it's music to us; Ha! Ha!" he laughs, "it's a good sign you won't faint."

Madame: "That's sensible, cheer her up," rolling up her sleeves and selecting a fine new birch rod of fresh green twigs, neatly tied with blue and pink silk ribbons.

"I shall give you slowly two dozens strokes, so as to finish the cutting open of the drawers, if possible by the last stroke."

Flora (in agonizing apprehension): "Ah! Oh! Oh! Horrible!"

Madame: "Try and bear it, dear, as well as you can; or scream if you like, it keeps the strength up better than sighs or moans."

She then draws the sides of the drawers up, and pins them in a pleat, on each side, so as to make them fit tightly across the devoted bum. Madame looks a perfect female devil, with her dark flashing eyes and saturnine beauty, which is sometimes terrible to behold, as with a kind of hissing, snake-like fierceness she counts "one—two—three—four" making a deliberate but slashing stroke at each word.

Sir Charles and poor Alice are both intent upon the

scene, the former forgetting to go on with his own victim, stares with gloating satisfaction, from Madame to Flora, and it is hardly possible to judge which figure impresses him most, the flogger or floggee; whilst his little daughter has slipped to the floor and is regarding the martyrdom of her sister with awe-stricken, sorrowful looks, and tears which her own sufferings have wrung from her.

"Five — six — seven" — whack — whack, — whack, sounds each blow causing Flora to plunge upon her tightened drawers which show no signs of yielding, till the ninth stroke, and at the tenth, a slight rent is plainly visible.

Poor Alice hides her eyes: Flora groans piteously: "Father! Oh! Mercy!"

Each stroke seems inflicted now, so as to slowly but surely tear open the drawers; at the sixteenth whack the rod shows evidence of the hard work it is doing, little bits come off at every blow, and Flora seems almost spent; but Madame skilfully directs the next as an undercut, so as to go right in under the crack of her bottom; exclaiming: "That's a reviver for you, Flora, and will help to split up the drawers better than banging all across your bottom; would you like another? there it is—eighteen."

The effect of these two cuts is so agonizing to the poor victim that she screams frantically.

"Oh! Ah! Ah! Madame! Oh! Father! Spare me! Finish! Do make haste! Oh! let me die!"

The concluding half-dozen strokes are given with undiminished vigour, and at the twenty-second, the drawers are all in tatters, bits of birch scratch and stick in the flesh, and Madame rapidly gives the last two blows, hideously laughing and calling Sir Charles to come and examine his daughter's bottom.

He does so minutely, pretending to be very much

affected at the sight.

"Flora, dear, how you must have suffered; there's scarcely any blood on your bottom, although the poor thing is dreadfully wealed and bruised; the drawers are in rags; it's all over red and swollen marks, and I can pick out little bits of the rod that have stuck in the skin. Tell me what you feel," kissing her bottom.

Flora: "Oh! Father! Dear Father! Save me now. If that woman has you in her power, make an effort to throw it off; how I have suffered; I burn all over, my thighs and bottom and—feel as if burnt with red hot irons."

Sir Charles: "Ah! my dear! Your little pussey is indeed hot and palpitating from the cruel usage; I can even see a drop or two of blood on the little pouting lips."

Here he frigs himself with one hand as he plays with her with the other.

Seeing and feeling her so excites him that he snatches up a riding whip and commences, slash—slash—slash, exclaiming:

"She's only been tickled yet; see what I can do to such an obstinate girl."

Flora shrieks: "Papa! Papa! have mercy, you'll kill me! Ah!-r-r-re! you must indeed be mad!" She gasps at the blows which cut so severely as almost to take her breath away. The blood begins to trickle down each cheek of her bottom.

Sir Charles (shouting loudly): "There's no mercy in me; you say I am murdering you, do you! Yes, I'll murder your bottom; I am mad am I?" cutting away with fearful energy; "but girl's bottoms have as many lives as cat's, as Coleman says in the 'Rodiad!' if but made of the proper sort of stuff, you really can't pitch into them enough."

One moment the victim seems nearly dead, but the

next cruel cut revives her, and she shrieks again and again with agony.

Madame, with a brutal laugh, remarks: "She's beginning to bleed nicely, now, how delicious it looks; it will do her good."

Sir Charles: "Yes, I feel as if I could drink it, the sight makes me wild with excitement."

Madame: "I thought you were dead to all such feelings."

Sir Charles: "You have indeed found the means to rejuvenate me; I feel a veritable satyr."

Madame: "There are many more ideas yet to be tried; I thought your case was so bad something much stronger would have to be resorted to."

During this short dialogue the father never relaxes the whipping of his daughter; the sight of her bleeding posteriors and the cries of exquisite pain, only excite him, as it would a tiger tearing his prey to pieces. Now seeing her just about to faint, he gives a tremendous slash with the riding whip, across her back, just below the shoulders, the end of the whip almost reaching her tender bosom, and leaving an abraded cut around under the armpit; he slashes again crying: "Die if you can, but this will revive you;" raising another tremendous weal, and drawing blood from her lacerated back.

Poor Flora screams in a heart-rending manner: "Papa! Papa! Oh! Mercy! now let me faint! The torments of Hell can't be so bad as this! Oh! Ah-r-r-r-e! Oh! My God! Oh!"

At this crisis Madame perceives a little foam on her lips, which she points out to Sir Charles, taking the whip from his hand to give her a little respite.

This sight raises their sensual excitement yet more and more; Sir Charles is getting quite wild. "Put on another pair of drawers," he cries, "and see me cut them wide open, yours was child's play to what mine will be."

Flora moans: "Oh! Oh! they won't let me go till I am quite dead."

Madame (producing a smaller sized pair than the last): "See there, these were made to fit Alice, but the tighter the better fun they make;" she then approaches the exhausted and almost fainting victim, giving her raw flesh two or three smart slaps, to wake her up and make her step into the fresh drawers, which cause excruciating agony, as they fit tightly everywhere and have been well peppered inside.

His daughter's agony only makes Sir Charles' enjoyment the greater and he hastily selects a whip which has three tails of knotted cords at the end. The first stroke is so painful the victim suddenly droops her head and fairly faints, hanging in an unconscious state, supported by her hands.

This obliges them to have recourse to a cold douche, and as she slowly comes round, some strong snuff is forced up her nostrils, causing her to sneeze violently. Madame also rubs her clitoris and the lips of her cunny with some chilies, which thoroughly awaken her by the smarting sensation they cause.

Scarcely allowing her fairly to recover, Sir Charles resumes again and raves like a lunatic.

"She shan't go to sleep again, the lazy little puss; I'll keep her awake."

The blows sound with a sharp whack on the wet drawers, which stick and fit so closely that they are soon stained with blood, which runs rapidly through the wet material.

Flora screams in greatest agony at each tremendous stroke, as they resound through the apartment; her whole figure quivers as the slashing cuts fall upon her devoted bottom; the drawers soon show marks of giving way.

Sir Charles: "You gave twenty-four whacks, Madame, but you may flay me alive if I don't cut them to pieces with a dozen."

Flora: "Oh! Ah! kill me quick and put me out of my misery."

Sir Charles: "You won't die; the bottom is not a vital part; cheer up, cheer up, Flora dear; don't groan so, scream properly, it's more cheerful. Ha! Ha! you'll live for many another good whipping."

The victim moans, sobs and cries appealingly to them all in turn.

Madame steadies Sir Charles a little, so the blows fall more deliberately, but in twelve or thirteen cuts the drawers are again wrecked and the raw, bare flesh exposed again to the fury of his attack; the terrible whip cutting into the flesh with a hissing sound, causing the blood to trickle down, down, down, lower and lower down her thighs, to the tops of her pretty stockings, the sight of which distracts him from her bottom, and saying "he will cut her stockings off too," the blows are now aimed lower down, first just on the garters, then especially on the pretty graceful calves of her legs.

Flora revived again, by this change of attack, screams with a terrible shrill agonized voice. "The fiend! my father! Oh! Oh! Ah-r-r-re! Will you never have mercy? Oh! Ah!"

These cries excite him still more and more, the thin silk of the stockings gives way at every swish; the bare flesh, showing terrible broken weals, the blood trickling down, even into her boots.

Madame: "What a sight; how exciting; how deliciously she's pickled; but stay, stay now;" stopping his frenzied arm.

"Come here, Alice," dragging the poor girl who is

almost dead with fright. "Now, kneel down and lick the blood off your sister's raw bottom."

The young girl sobs with pity and terror combined; Madame, passing her hand over the bleeding surface, smears it over Alice's face, saying: "There, there; taste how nice it is."

Too frightened and horrified to resist, Alice, who has nothing on but her stockings and boots, kneels behind her sister and tries to accomplish the disgusting task; but the sight of her temptingly bent bottom is too much for Sir Charles who instantly gives her a severe cut with his whip.

Alice writhes so beautifully with speechless agony, showing her blood and tear-stained countenance, that Sir Charles insists on flogging her as well.

"Madame," he cries, "put on her drawers, and then tie her up, back to the post, and her legs well stretched out."

Madame, with fiendish delight, pounces on the poor girl, fixes her as required, and, giving several sharp, malicious pinches on her bottom and thighs, leaves her to the mercy of the whip.

Sir Charles (with an exulting laugh): "Ha! Ha! How I love you Alice, dear; I won't make your bottom so sore as Flora's." Saying which he whips her first across the hips, causing her to scream: "Oh! Oh! Ah! Father! Mercy! Mercy! Oh!"

Sir Charles again: "Ha! Ha! mine's love without mercy; the more I love the more I shall whack you, my dear."

Alice: "Oh! Ah! Ah! Oh! Let me go, I can't. Oh! I can't bear it;" as he cuts several times with underhand strokes between her thighs right up to her delicate and almost hairless little slit; drops of blood stain her drawers and she writhes and screams from the terrible pain.

At last, fearing she may faint, Madame interposes, turns her face to the post, and having fitted herself with a huge godemiche, tears open her drawers behind, saying: "Now, Sir Charles see how she will enjoy this. You, Flora, wake up and see what your loving Papa will do for you presently."

Madame: "Hold well open, or Papa will use his whip again."

Then taking some cold cream from a pot, she anoints Alice's burning little bottom hole, forcing in her finger, and working it about.

"Stand still, girl, or Sir Charles will slash you," she threatens, as the tender orifice shrinks from the rough attack of her finger.

Alice: "Oh! Oh! You're hurting me so, with your finger."

Madame: "Little fool, that's nothing—only to prepare the way."

Withdrawing her finger, the beautiful pink little hole contracts again and leaves a very small mark as the Frenchwoman presents the well-greased head of her godemiche, directing it, as well as she can, to the orifice and pushing hard, to effect an entrance, but without success.

Madame strikes her nails suddenly into the tender flesh of the poor girl, and as she recoils from the pain, thrusts again, pinching and nipping in front, to make the victim shove back her bottom.

Madame: "I'll get into you, if your hole is no larger than a tobacco pipe; push back, you little cochon, and draw your breath," pinching and nipping her breasts.

Alice: "Ah! Ah! Horrible, disgusting. Oh! you'll split my bottom!"

Madame: "So I will before I've done;" forcing the head of the godemiche in a little way.

Alice: "You awful beast let me go! Oh! Oh! Father,

save me! Mercy!"

Madame (thrusting her fingers into the bleeding crack in front and getting more angry as Alice wriggles her bottom to escape the torture): "Shove back, you little devil, or I'll tear your slit open!"

Alice (shrieking with the fearful pain): "Ah-r-r-r-re! Oh! Oh! God have mercy!"

She screams again and again, as Madame slowly forces the awful instrument up into her body; the little hole, torn and bleeding, yet throbs and contracts, so as to increase the horrible rending sensation; the victim moans piteously, her head droops and she swoons away, so as to defy all their efforts to revive her.

Then Sir Charles in a paroxysm of lustful rage, attacks poor Flora again with his whip till the blood pours afresh, the sight of which renders both of them furious with erotic passion, but Madame, slightly more prudent than Sir Charles, advises him to stop or he'll have no bottom to enculer.

Flora: "Oh! spare me that humiliation, dear father; whip me to death rather."

Sir Charles (lifting his shirt so as fully to expose himself to her view): "You saw Madame Josephine ravish Alice's bottom with her Parisian godemiche, but that's nothing to the pleasure I shall derive from forcing my living instrument up your fundus, Flora, dear!"

Flora: "Oh! be merciful, pity my deplorable state; see, Alice is nearly dead; look, she's only just coming round now, after her long faint."

Madam: "Fainting never kills; it gives a little rest, that's all. Alice is just in time to be useful," pouring a cordial down her throat, and also giving some to Flora. "That will give you courage."

Alice is now made to crawl, half fainting as she is, to

the right position, first take his swollen and bursting priapus and moisten it in her mouth, then kneel behind him, lick his bottom and handle his testicles. This so excites Sir Charles that, taking hold of poor Flora's raw buttocks, he tears the bleeding cheeks apart and thrusts at the blood-stained entrance which shrinks from his attack, but in vain. Madame, also kneeling down, pinches and torments her poor pussey, pricking the little mossy mount all over with a hair pin, to make her properly meet Sir Charles' advance in the rear.

Flora (with awful screams): "My God! My God! Oh! Oh Father! Oh Madame! Mercy! Ah-r-re! Mercy! I must die this time! Ah! Oh! My bottom's splitting!"

The satyr of a father only raves and gloats over her agony, exclaiming:

"That's good, scream and shriek away, my girls, my prick is hard as iron. How true it is when the blood is so heated and maddened that 'a standing prick has no conscience'!"

He pushes with fury, till the head of his instrument is fairly lodged within the tightly contracting sphincter muscle; she shrieks and plunges with the agony, whilst he continues to thrust forward, without even drawing the least back, for fear of losing his advantage. Madame tortures her in front, and then applies cold cream to the shaft of Sir Charles' pego, to facilitate its entrance.

Flora, all the while screaming again and again for pity, for mercy, and bidding Alice good bye, as she was dying; just as Sir Charles, bursting through all obstacles, tears and rends his way to a complete insertion.

She faints, but the muscular contractions of the anus are so delicious that in a wild shooting thrill of ecstasy, he seems to spend his inmost life into her vitals, quite exhausting him for the moment; but the long tension of previous excitement keeps his instrument as hard as ever; whilst the continued pulsations and delicious contractions speedily bring back all his lustful sensations. With haggard looks and starting eyes he greedily swallows two or three bumpers of champagne, sighing: "Oh! for some one to kill; what voluptuous sensations it must create!"

Madame's real character now comes out. She whispers to him:

"Why not? You have another beautiful daughter; who not let my Augustine bring her in and help us! The greater extremities we go to and the more prolonged the excitement, we shall find these enjoyments continually enhanced in their exquisite and voluptuous sensations. The beautifully and fully developed Maud in the full power of her youthful virginity, humiliated, crying, bleeding and fainting from time to time, will afford you all these erotic joys."

Sir Charles, mad with lust and cruelty, orders Augustine to be called and take away Flora and Alice, who are dismissed with an assurance of a repetition of the fun, as soon as they are recovered.

Scene The Second

Enter Augustine, the servant, with Maud.

The fresh victim is a beautiful blonde of eighteen, light brown hair tinged with gold, large blue eyes, rather above the medium height, very plump and fair; she has a nervous suspicious look on her face, but Sir Charles (who has enveloped himself in a dressing gown), and Madame receive her with an air of assumed gravity

Maud: "Oh! Father. Why have you sent for me to this place?"

(Taking in at a glance the various appointments for punishment.)

"I have missed my poor sisters and for a long time have been hearing some indistinct cries of pain. Have you been punishing them?"

Sir Charles: "They too well deserve what Madame has inflicted on them for their contemptuous behaviour to her. Maud, you too, have not shown the respect properly due to your governess."

Maud: "Ah! Dear Father! I am not the same as my younger sisters; you know I am to be married before long, and have never been under Madame Josephine."

Madame: "Sir Charles, her answer plainly shows how I am treated; it is her example which makes the others worse."

Sir Charles: "Are you willing to make a humble submission to Madame, and beg her pardon for your previous disrespect?"

Maud (faltering and blushing all over with indignation): "Oh! No!—Dear Father—why did you bring us all to this desolate place to put that woman over us? I—I—am sure Sir William Pokingham—your own choice of a husband for me—would blame me if I did."

Sir Charles: "Damme! What has Sir William to do with my family arrangements? Make your submission proud Miss or we shall know how to subdue your obstinacy. Now; yes or no?"

Maud: "To you, dear Father, but never to Madame Josephine!"

Madame locks the door, and at a motion from Sir Charles she and the servant catch hold of the young lady, who, with flashing eyes, and indignant look, wrenches herself from their grasp, but only to be more firmly seized the next moment, for Augustine is a stout, strong wench, of determined character. Maud's delicate, sensitive feelings revolt at the idea of a personal struggle, and she now allows herself to be secured to the ladder, her face suffused with the flush of shame and humiliation as they fasten her hands well above her head.

Sir Charles: "Strip her to the buff, we'll see what a little mild discipline will effect."

Maud: "Oh! Father, Father, spare me! Punish me yourself; don't let them touch me! Oh! Oh! Infamous!" she cries, as they tear off her beautiful silk dress and proceed to slip off her white petticoats, so as to leave her standing in only her flannel petticoat, corset and drawers, the latter of which are rather long, and come well below the knees, showing the richly embroidered ends, the well turned ankles and beautiful feet, in delicate high-heeled boots.

There she stands, the picture of indignation, her face, neck and heaving bosom crimsoned at the burning sense of shame.

Madame: "We won't expose her too much, Sir Charles, unless you insist upon it; perhaps we may not have to degrade her so much if she will but express her regret."

Sir Charles: "As you please, Madame; it only shows your thoughtful kindness."

Augustine and Madame now turn up and secure her skirts, so as to fully expose all her posterior arrangements, showing how well her expanded hips fill out the drawers which fit rather tightly across her bottom.

Madame: "Now, Augustine, just open the drawers properly behind, and put the tail of her chemise well out of the way.'

Maud (as she feels her flesh exposed): "Oh! Oh! How indecent; how shameful!"

Madame now arms herself with a good and elegantly tied rod of birch and gently gives one or two preliminary switches, so as gradually to warm the parts, without much hurt, saying:

"Miss Maud, I'm sorry to have to punish such a great girl as you and hope you will soon submit to your father's wishes."

Maud: "Oh! No, no! Never to you Madame," biting her lips to suppress her emotion.

Madame: "Does that do you good?" giving a smarter stroke, which raises a long red mark across her loins.

Sir Charles: "Do your duty, Madame; none of your soft-heartedness!"

Maud: "Oh Father! Spare me! Oh! Oh!" as she gets a heavy smarting stroke.

Madame: "Your obstinacy must be cured; take that and that," giving two cuts lower down, across the thighs, causing great pain to the victim, who suppresses her cries and merely sighs at each blow. "She's obstinate and foolish to try my temper. Excuse me, Sir Charles, the hussey must be subdued."

Whack — whack — whack — fall three more tremendous cuts, bruising and wealing the fine plump bottom in every direction.

Maud: "Ah! Ah! Ah-r-r-re! You're murdering me! Oh!"

Madame: "Will you beg my pardon, and set your sisters a better example of respect to me in the future?" still cutting away with the rod, many of the marks showing blows which go right in between her tender thighs.

Maud (desperately): "Never! A-r-r-re! Never! I'll die first!" biting her lips in agony till they bled.

The poor girl is obstinate, although almost fainting. She suppresses all her cries, as well as possible, to avoid giving her tormenters any satisfaction.

Slight drops of blood ooze from the bruised flesh, and Madame's fury gets greater and greater as she feels herself tiring and the victim obstinate.

The blows fall in a pitiless shower, breaking the rod into numberless small fragments some of which scratch and stick in the flesh; but without avail for Maud suffers the most excruciating pain with only suppressed sobs and moans and finally baffles all Madame's rage by fainting just as she throws away the stump of the rod and asks for another.

"What a resolute girl," says Madame, grinding her teeth, "but we shall soon revive her and have further satisfaction, till her proud spirit is broken."

Sir Charles: "Strip her naked so when she revives she will find herself without a rag to cover her."

This is speedily effected and unloosening her hands they pour champagne down her throat and she is soon brought round by blowing her face with a strong pair of bellows and sprinkling water all over her naked body. She wakes up in horror just as Sir Charles, with cruel laughter, is blowing her virgin crack.

Sir Charles, laughing: "Ha! Ha! Ha! That's the best way to freshen them up. Now Madame, put on a new pair of drawers and let Augustine try her hand at cutting them open. Fix her to the post."

Maud: "Oh! Father! Father! How can you be so cruel? Oh! Spare me now!"

Sir Charles: "Shriek away, my daughter; it's the sweetest music to me."

Madame: "Aye; she'll find out how to cry for mercy yet!"

Augustine, now the victim is once more secured and dressed in a fresh pair of drawers, tight fitting behind and only open in front, stands ready with a whipping instrument made of many thongs or small strips of leather, fastened on a handle. She is a fine, dark, young Frenchwoman of five-and-twenty, and, having thrown aside her outside dress, her well rounded arms and strong legs encased in red silk stockings, indicate great strength.

Madame: "Now, Augustine, let us see you've not forgotten your business; but I will do all the speaking and give directions, if necessary."

The "cocotte" lays on heartily, with sparkling eyes and heightened colour, attesting the pleasure she herself feels. The strokes fall regularly at intervals of about half a minute, cutting and rapidly damaging the thin materials of the drawers, which soon begin to show evidences of the laceration going on, spots of blood stain appearing all over their surface.

The poor girl writhes in her agony, and at last, as if to relieve the pain a little, screams wildly for:

"Mercy! Ah! Ah! Oh! You're cutting me to pieces. Mercy! Oh! I'll do all you want!"

Madame: "Will you beg my pardon now? Ha! Ha! There's nothing like leather!"

Maud: "Oh! Father! Pity! Mercy! Ah-r-r-r!" as she now feels the cuts on her bare flesh; the drawers are in rags and each stroke cuts the skin, and her crimsoned bottom runs with blood, which drips all down her thighs.

Madam: "What a beautiful sight, how exciting to see the young virgin blood!"

Sir Charles: "Lay on! Lay on! Ha! Ha! Ha! You French devil. Cut into her beautiful bottom!"

Maud: "Oh God! Oh God! I am going! Oh! Oh! Mercy!"

Madame: "Not yet! Not yet, Miss! Cut her underneath."

Augustine, flushed with excitement is only too willing to prolong the poor girl's agony and cuts her so as to reach the delicate mossed mount in front, scoring her thighs, and drawing more blood at every stroke.

Poor Maud, in horrible agony, screams and yells for mercy.

"Ah-r-r-re! My God! Do spare me! Will no one pity me?" She moans, dropping her head with exhaustion, failing more and more at each cruel stroke, till at last, Madame, in an excess of excitement, snatches the leather whip away, orders the servants to loosen her hands and help in laying her across her knee.

Almost spent, the poor girl is nearly incapable of resistance, but Madame, having turned up her skirts, so that she may experience the pleasure of feeling the struggling victim on her own bare thighs.

Maud, mad with pain and her great humiliation, longing for some slight revenge on the cruel Frenchwoman, succeeds in making her teeth meet in the exposed flesh. With a sharp cry of fury and rage Madame grasps the poor bleeding bottom with both hands, digging her nails into the raw surface, whilst Augustine strikes her on the face with her clenched fist, to make her loose her hold, which she retains in spite of them, until her mouth is forced open, having copious signs of her enemy's blood upon her lips.

Madame furious at such an unforeseen punishment

now slaps the poor, mutilated bottom with tremendous savageness, each blow resounding through the room—slap—slap—slap—slap.

Maud is more dead than alive; too feeble to scream; she only moans weaker and weaker till she is past consciousness.

As soon as they are assured that she is beyond feeling, they lay her on the floor and apply various restoratives, especially a strong cordial, which is poured down her throat, plenty of water and also wind from the bellows, and as she slowly recovers, Sir Charles bends over her and kisses her bruised bottom, wipes her bleeding nose, saying:

"Poor darling, how these fiends have murdered you; I'll save you from them; they shan't touch you again."

Thus assured, she slowly revives, when Sir Charles, maddened with erotic excitement, makes them dress her in another pair of tight-fitting drawers and tie her to the post.

He now takes a regular cat-o-nine tails, a fearful weapon of knotted cords, and begins to slash her across her bare shoulders; each cut goes through the beautiful white skin, and raises innumerable weals; the blood streams down and saturates the drawers; his blows gradually work downwards, across the loins, the poor victim screaming and moaning.

"Ah! Oh! Oh! What a horrible death to die!"

Sir Charles, beside himself with excitement, throws off his dressing gown and stands fully exposed to his awe-stricken, degraded and almost dying daughter, the front of his shirt all stained with poor Flora's blood; his belly and thighs all ensanguined and seared; and above all his frightful, fiery-looking pego distended and swollen, in the highest state of lust.

Poor Maud shuts her eyes to keep out the horrible sight.

He now attacks her bottom with fearful energy, cutting the drawers to rags and making streams of blood run down her thighs, and even to her stockings and boots; the cordial she has taken keeps her from going off, but she moans more feebly every moment.

Sir Charles is madder than ever, exclaiming:

"Oh! Oh! I must die in her; whip us both to death if you can!" then throws aside the cat and springs forward to "enculer" the bleeding wreck of raw flesh before him.

Madame assists to direct his inflamed instrument in the right way and help the insertion with a little cold cream.

This unexpected attack quite recovers the drooping Maud; she screams with agony and horror.

"My God! Oh! Mercy! you're rending me in pieces!" But the furious maniac thrusts till he quickly gains a partial entrance then with redoubled energy fairly splits his way through the bleeding lacerated orifice of her delicate anus. She screams and writhes, which gives him exquisite pleasure.

Madame and Augustine thrash them both with new rods, Sir Charles on his hardy bottom and Maud across her hips, belly or mount.

The victim swoons, but the two women hold her up, and Sir Charles, clasping her firmly behind, steadies himself so as to feel the ecstatic pulsations of the contracting muscles, which speedily draw from him the very essence of his life.

At last he withdraws, exhausted, but with a still distended priapus, and raging with maddening excitement, declaring "he has not half done yet."

Madame tries to restrain him a little, but the sight of poor Maud slowly recovering makes him furious to use the whip once more. They secure her, nearly gone as she is, to the ladder, spread-eagled by her hands and feet, pour more cordial down her gasping throat, throw water over her, and then Sir Charles rushes to his victim, dealing fearful cuts everywhere he could see a bit of flesh not already scored with the lash, cutting round her neck, arms and ribs, making her one frightful mass of weals and blood-stained flesh.

She is now too weak to writhe and struggle, but moans, fainter and fainter; her head drops lifeless and the spirit is really gone.

"Dead! Dead! Dead!" yelled Sir Charles, still striking in his frantic excitement, and drops to the floor in a swoon.

END OF VOL. I.

Part the Second

New Victims Secured

A few days after the events narrated in the previous part, Sir Charles and Madame Josephine are consulting together in his sitting room, how to explain away the disappearance of their sister to Flora and Alice, and also how further to carry out, if possible, more and more erotic ideas.

Sir Charles: "I have settled in my mind that Maud must be supposed to have run away to escape your surveillance; that is a very easy excuse, and you should instruct Augustine to break the news to them. No one but ourselves can possibly know how we have disposed of her but my God! what a height of voluptuous excitement it raised in me!

"Poor Maud! Poor Maud! (shedding tears) yet I should do it again; my fatherly love only seems to heighten my excitement, and add to the blissful sensations I felt; it is impossible to ever forget them, and she's only gone to Heaven a little sooner than the others. Poor dear!"

Madame: "Your plan is a good one, to account for Maud, but how are we to get fresh victims to keep up the excitement; natives of this country won't do; we don't understand their language, and there would be little pleasure without understanding their cries."

Sir Charles: "I think someone should go to Constantinople to seek Maud; at least, if I go that would be my excuse; you will take care of all in my absence, and get the two girls quite well again; perhaps I could find some English or French ladies there, and carry them off in some way; money will do anything."

Madame: "You could buy Circassian slaves, if no others are to be had; but the cholera has made great ravages there lately; you might be able to hear of some orphans if you represent yourself as a philanthropic, and desirous of befriending and taking home to their own country, some one who may have been left in distress."

Sir Charles starts for the Turkish capital, and in about three weeks a letter comes by courier to Madame as follows:

"Dear Madame Josephine—

"After several days' search I heard of a Greek family whose father had just been carried off by the epidemic; the mother died three years ago, and the father, M. Demreti has been a most prosperous merchant until a few months ago, when his correspondents at Odessa and Galatz, in the corn trade (for he was a great speculator in grain) became involved in difficulties, which also brought him to ruin; this reduced him to such a despondent state of mind that when the cholera seized him he rapidly succumbed to the disease, leaving his four daughters, of twenty-four, seventeen, thirteen and ten years old respectively entirely unprovided for; their only friends and relations being uncles in London and Liverpool, who were estranged from their brother many years ago.

"You may be sure I did not allow the grass to grow under my feet; so I soon called upon the orphans as an old friend of their father's and explained to them that I had only a little business to transact in Asia Minor and if they would entrust themselves to me, we would travel overland to Smyrna, doing my business on the way, and embark there for England, where I was assured their uncles would suitably provide for them, and that otherwise I would take care they should come to no harm.

"Very few objections were raised to my proposal, and they only required a few days to settle their affairs; I have furnished them with money to fit themselves out in the best fashions of the day.

"Another person will return with me, an Englishwoman of about thirty, who has spent many years of her life in the Sultan's seraglio; but at last finding herself quite neglected for other favourites, made her escape a few days ago, and hearing of me, applied for help; she is named Lucidora and so interested me with her exciting disclosures of harem life that I engaged her to assist you in our divertisements, as she is thoroughly up to the business, and we shall want help to keep our increased household in order.

"The young ladies are very beautiful and named Haidee, Veneria, Sophia and Melissa, the last a particularly sweet little thing. You may expect me with my troupe in four or five days.

> "Yours truly,
> "Charles Dacre."

Madame makes every preparation for the young ladies; Flora and Alice, now convalescent, are informed of the expected arrivals and cautioned not to mention anything about punishment on pain of their Papa's displeasure.

Alice: "Oh! Madame Josephine, Augustine says

Maud has run away from you."

Madame: "So she has but Sir Charles will recover her and punish her in some way; if not personally at least she will never get a shilling from her father, whatever distress she may be in."

Flora: "But Madame, he will never punish us so again, will he, if we are obedient to you?"

Madame: "You must take care; your Papa is a strange man and has curious ideas of the proper discharge of his duty, and the discipline to be maintained in his house; he has been lately converted to his present notions by some curious treatises on Flagellation."

Alice: "It's so dull without Maud; how wrong it was of her to run away from us all just because Papa insists that Madame is to be over every one. It will be pleasant if the Demetris are nice girls; will he punish them?"

Madame: "Yes, that he will, if they give him cause; you must tell them we are only staying here for a month or two, as Sir Charles is interested in some mines close by in the neighbourhood, and inspecting the country to see if it is possible to cut a canal to the sea."

Flora: "Ah! Madame, how strange it seems to feel so well and happy again, after our dreadful punishment, it does not seem credible that it could have been real, such torture, as we went through, and yet now we're alive and sound as ever."

Madame: "Sir Charles gets beside himself, when you put him out so; the sight of your blood excites him so, he knows not what he is doing, and in his fury, he would kill anyone who disobeyed him."

Flora: "How awful; yet now the dreadful scenes, seems to have a strange fascination for my thoughts."

Alice: "And so it is with me; the pain and agony were

fearful, and yet at times I felt an ecstatic thrill, impossible to be imagined."

Thus prepared, every one welcomes Sir Charles and his protégés. On their arrival the new young ladies are introduced to Madame, as their future governess, Mademoiselle Haidee a splendid dark girl, with the true Grecian type of countenance, arches her eyebrows, with a repudiating expression of surprise, as Sir Charles explicitly informs them all "that Madame is very strict, in her domestic arrangements, and must be deferred to in every respect."

Haidee: "But Sir Charles, you're not going to stay long in this out-of-the-way place I hope?"

Sir Charles: "Oh! No! Only a week or two weeks, till I can see my way clear about investing in the mines."

Haidee: "I am sure we shall love your dear daughters, and if Flora and Alice only keep us right, we shan't be much trouble to your housekeeper."

Madame soon finds an opportunity to inform Sir Charles that he will have to begin with Haidee, who is so imperious and self-willed; nothing is good enough for her and she has not the slightest respect for any of the regulations of the house.

Sir Charles is only too anxious to renew the experiences of the torture chamber, so they arrange for a séance the very next morning, when the high-spirited young lady is to be invited to a private conference with Sir Charles and Madame.

During the forenoon of the ensuing day, a favourable circumstance gives Madame an excellent pretext for attempting to curb Haidee's self will; the little Melissa, bathed in tears, appeals to Madame Josephine from the eldest sister's severity, having been well boxed on the ears for breaking a small looking glass, in that young lady's boudoir.

Madame expostulates with Haidee about showing so

much temper over an accident and pities the little sufferer, telling Haidee "she ought to be ashamed of such cruelty to her own little sister."

Haidee, flashing up with anger, retorts, "she has a right to punish the little minx, who is always in mischief."

Madame: "Sir Charles never permits such things in his house; I have to report any offence to him before it can be punished."

Haidee (indignantly): "Then I suppose you will report me for my hasty temper?"

Madame: "Indeed I think you had better speak to Sir Charles about it this evening in the lecture room when he is ready to see you."

Haidee: "It is quite a matter of indifference; neither you nor Sir Charles has a right to lecture me; I am sorry we put ourselves under an obligation to him; it would have been better for us if I had accepted the offer of marriage that was made me and so provided a home for my sisters as well as myself."

Madame: "It is useless for me to talk to such a proud young lady; Sir Charles must see to his own dignity."

After dinner Sir Charles retires to consult with Madame Josephine in what is now called the lecture room.

Sir Charles: "How do you propose to proceed with Mademoiselle Haidee?"

Madame: "You will find her very determined and desperate; there's something so self-asserting about the girl."

Sir Charles: "The more fun for us."

Madame: "Can you depend on Lucidora to help us?"

Sir Charles: "Oh! She'll be all you could wish; she can tell us some of her experiences in the seraglio."

Madame: "Are they really racy?"

Sir Charles: "I should think so; she's had to eat her own excrement, for punishment, and tells me that every new addition to the harem is at first thoroughly subdued and humiliated by having to eat some of the Sultan's; we must bring this girl to her senses in something of that way; by Jove! how she will like it!"

Madame: "You'll find rare fun from the first; it won't be so easy to get her stripped."

Sir Charles: "Well, let us begin; I've already got a slight rise from your conversation, the idea is so stimulating. I can already see, in imagination, the scenes we shall go through. I'm sure I'm mad upon this point if sane in everything else; all people have some peculiar madness of their own, but very few are aware of it. Now I'll ring for Lucidora to introduce this beautiful Haidee, the veritable 'Belle Helene.'"

The splendid Greek girl now enters, with a slightly flushed face, and firmly set lips; as if resolved to assert her rights, but, as she hears the key turn in the lock behind her, and her eyes take in all the castigatory arrangements of the apartment, she turns suddenly pale, then again flushes up with evident indignation.

Madame: "Allow me, Sir Charles, to introduce to you a rather high-spirited young lady, who repudiates all interference when I expostulate with her, upon her cruel attack upon her little sister Melissa, who she slapped and beat unmercifully this morning for a petty little accident."

Sir Charles: "I'm astonished to hear this of you Haidee; you ought to be as a mother to your sisters; if you don't show mercy, how can you expect it yourself!"

Haidee: "Indeed, Sir, I don't see why Madame should have interfered with me; the child deserved it."

Sir Charles: "No one can punish in this house without my consent; you will soon have to be punished yourself if you do not respect Madame Josephine; did your parents never chastise you?"

Haidee: "No indeed it would not be good for any one to lay hands on me;" flushing more and more from her rising indignation.

Madame: "You see her haughty spirit, Sir Charles; she respects no one!"

Sir Charles (taking a fine freshly tied birch in his hand): "Ha! Ha! young lady; did you never taste any thing of this kind? Don't you know what it's for? Well, then, it's just to tickle up the bare bottoms of proud young Misses like you, who have never known restraint. Come now, apologize to Madame, and beg pardon for your unfeeling brutality to little Melissa."

Haidee (her eyes flashing fire and almost beside herself with indignant shame): "Brutality indeed, Sir Charles, I'll do no such thing; it's your own speech which rather ought to be termed so; to speak so indelicately to a modest young lady; you shall never punish me in that way."

Sir Charles: "We shall see, Miss Lucifer; your pride shall be brought down; a well-scored smarting bum will make you reflect and beg for pardon. Once more will you apologize or not?"

Haidee: "How degrading! How shameful," hiding her face in her hands. Then as if ashamed of the action, stamps with her foot in a rage, exclaiming: "No! never, never, never! There, Sir! I and my sisters will soon relieve you of any anxiety about our future guardianship; there seems something infernal in all this; who are you, man? What trap have we fallen into?"

Sir Charles: "Come, come, Miss Termagant, you'll soon find out who I am. Now if you won't apologize, just kiss this rod, and kneel down, and ask Madame to do her duty for your good. Ha! Ha! Ha!" laughs Sir Charles at his own joke, and holding out the rod towards the indignant girl.

Haidee, with sudden energy, snatches it away and tramples it under her feet, exclaiming: "So much for your rod, Sir." She turns her back upon him.

Sir Charles: "You may turn your back, but know, proud, obstinate, cruel, wilful, scornful girl as you are, we have means to bring down your haughty spirit; I will just tell you what you will have to feel before you leave this room; look around and take notice of all the pretty little things here ready for your amusement. You don't like birch; do you like nettles? Do you like holly? Do you like a lady's riding whip? Do you like a whalebone whip? We have also a nice cat-o-nine tails of knotted cords, if you are extra obstinate; you will be stripped to your petticoats, your skirts turned up and that proud bottom of yours well castigated till the blood bursts from the red weals; then you shall be stripped naked, tied to the ladder yonder, flogged with nettles and holly from your thighs; then you will be turned fronting us and with pincers every hair of your beautiful what-do-you-call-it shall be pulled out. Ha! Ha! Ha! Well make you tell us its proper name yourself. Now, you know what to expect; Madame, let Lucidora do her duty, and prepare the young lady; help her if necessary; it's too late to think of mercy now."

Haidee: "Oh! Oh! Oh! Heavens! Where am I? What insults, what infamy, what wretches!" as Lucidora approaches; "off, woman, off I say! Touch me at your peril!"

Now ensues a desperate scene.

Haidee is well formed, supple and fired with desperate resolution; Lucidora and Madame are scratched and torn in their endeavours to tie her to the post, and had it not been for some timely assistance from Sir Charles (who, seizing a favourable opportunity, managed to handcuff her wrists) she would have beaten them both off.

Thus, comparatively helpless, she is dragged to the whipping tree in a terribly torn and dishevelled state, almost fainting from her fierce resistance, but still indignant and resolute.

"Ha! Ha!" laughs Sir Charles.

"Trust me for coming to the rescue. By Jove! you two women were no use at all; you would have both been well beaten; look at your torn dresses and scratched faces. Madame and you Lucidora are as good as looking glasses for each other."

Madame (grinding her teeth): "Sacre Diable! She shall rue it finely; let me handle the rod, Sir Charles?"

Sir Charles: "With pleasure, Madame; my turn will come bye and bye. Lucidora, go on removing her rags."

Haidee kicks furiously, but her efforts are fruitless in resisting the removal of her torn dress and petticoats; her palpitating, heaving bosom is fully displayed in all its rounded beauty, the crimson flush of shame extending over the exposed parts of her neck and bust, which also, as well as her beautiful plump arms, show the severe marks of nipping and grasping fingers; her upper garments are reduced to a handsomely worked corset and embroidered drawers, the latter exhibiting every indication of beautiful proportions from the loins to the knees.

Sir Charles (rapturously feeling her plump bottom through the drawers): "What splendid buttocks, how firm and elastic to the touch; let us see the beautiful skin."

Opening the drawers and pulling up her chemise, he passes his hand between her thighs and caresses the silky soft hair of her mount in front.

"This is the thing, what do you call it, Miss Haidee; we want to know the proper name!"

Haidee (in agony as he plucks the hair): "You vile fellow; how dare you, even when I am helpless; how disgusting!"

Sir Charles: "I call it awfully nice; we want the right name and not your reflections, my dear."

Haidee: "How dare you say 'my dear' to me, you odious man?"

Madame is now ready with a fine new birch, ornamented with dark blue and gold ribbons; she stands behind the captive girl, her flashing dark eyes and heaving bosom plainly attesting her revengeful eagerness to begin on the devoted bottom before her, as she says:

"Trust me, Sir Charles, to make her speak up. Now, you proud, self-willed, rebellious girl look out; the sooner you beg for mercy the better for you. How do you like that!" swishing a sharp stroke of the rod, on the narrow exposed surface where the drawers had been opened a little by Sir Charles; this is followed up by three or four harder blows which raise bright red weals on the rosy surface, and make the courageous girl wince at every stroke.

Madame: "Will you be so cruel to your little sister again?" increasing the force of the blows.

Haidee (with indignant rage): "Spare your words and do your work, you wretches!"

Madame: "What a fine spirit! Does your pretty bottom tingle and smart yet; it looks rosy enough?"

Haidee: "Oh! Oh! Oh! to be so exposed and degraded! What insults!"

Madame (giving a fearful undercut, right up to the lips of her crack): "Do you call that degrading and insulting? It will have a warming effect."

Haidee: "Ah! Ah! Ah-r-r-re! disgusting!" then getting another in the same place: "Oh! Oh! God deliver me from these murdering people!"

Sir Charles: "Make her give you her opinion on the discipline of the birch."

Madame: "Now, Miss Imperious, speak up; don't be afraid to say anything that comes to your mind," cutting and wealing the poor girl's bottom at every stroke.

Sir Charles: "Take the lady's riding whip; that's the thing to make them speak up."

Lucidora hands Madame a very smart, pliant lady's whip and the latter evidently piqued at the great firmness of the victim, gives a first slash right across the delicate shoulders, raising a long red bruise, from which the blood is almost ready to start; then another and another slash, one of which causes a dark weal on the tender globe of her right breast and brings an involuntary scream of deepest anguish from the sufferer: "Ah! Ah! Oh! how it cuts! I shall be murdered! Oh!"

Madame: "'Ah! Ha! you can feel, can you, a little; try that and that," slashing poor Haidee across the face with pitiless cuts each one of which leaves a long red mark.

"I'll take the proud, haughty look off your face," then across the month and lips, raising a great swelling. "Now you can smile scornfully."

Haidee jerks and twists in every possible manner, shutting her eyes so as not to see her tormentors, and clenching her teeth in agony.

Sir Charles: "She's shutting her eyes; put a tight pair of drawers on her, and let Lucidora wake her up by cutting them open; Lucidora, you must do it in less than two dozen cuts."

Sir Charles now swallows a bumper of champagne and Lucidora and Madame follow his example; he offers a glass to Haidee and presents it to her lips, who, faint and gasping as she is, is anxious to allay her thirst from anybody's hands, but just as her parched mouth anticipates the cooling draught, with a scornful laugh: "Ha! Ha! Ha!" he dashes it in her face.

The drawers and every vestige of clothing except stockings and boots is now torn off, and poor Haidee, manacled as she is, stands exposed to the libidinous gaze of her tyrants; face, neck and bosom scored with angry looking weals, her bottom also well flushed and marked. She seems to blush all over her body at the shameful degradation and keeps her eyes firmly closed so as not to see the enjoyment of her persecutors.

"What a splendid white belly; what a delicious looking mount; what a glossy black soft silky hair over her pussey," exclaims Sir Charles in delight. "Make haste with those drawers, I want to enjoy the graceful contortions of her beautifully modelled body."

Madame: "Lucidora, before you fix those drawers on, just give her a gentle bottom frig; Miss Haidee must learn what that is, and taste and lick your finger."

Lucidora, approaching behind, wets two fingers of her right hand in her mouth, applies them one to each orifice of her virgin bottom and pussey, and, being a skilful manipulator, soon has both well inserted, so as speedily to create a delicious sense of lubricity; the parts having been so well excited and warmed by the previous discipline.

The poor girl is almost beside herself from the novelty of the sensations she now experiences for the first time, which with the confusion, shame and sense of degradation, cause infinite delight to Sir Charles, as he watches the variations of her countenance, whilst she is still ashamed to open her eyes.

"See how she likes it, Madame. Ah! Lucidora, how beautifully you use your fingers; keep yourself aside, so as not to obscure my view more than you can help. Tell us, Haidee, how do you feel; let us know when it's coming" exclaims Sir Charles.

Haidee (with indignation, writhing her bottom in spite of herself): "Oh! Oh! Oh! Horrible! Disgusting! Why do you torment me so and take advantage of my natural feelings; what refinement of cruelty!" Writhing and twisting with the excitement and unable to prevent the profuse spending which lubricates Lucidora's fingers and hand all over, with a slight mixture of sperm and excrement.

Madame: "Now, let her taste it, and lick it off your fingers; now, Miss Arrogance, put out your tongue and suck it in;" the fingers are pressed on her firmly closed lips and wiped across them and all over her face: "There, that will do, she can't help getting a good taste!"

They now lift up her feet, one at a time, and put her legs into the fresh drawers, which have no opening behind and fit tightly over her well rounded buttocks.

Madame: "Now cut away; as I count the blows, lay on well, or the whip won't cut them open as it ought— one, two, three—slash, slash, slash—fall the cuts, with a cracking sound. Poor Haidee is almost dead with pain; it seems as if each stroke was carving her bottom like a round of beef; she shrieks: "Ah! Oh! Oh God! have mercy save me! Oh! Oh!"

Madame: "She can speak at last; then taking up a bunch of holly, proceeds to flog all over and around the mons veneris of the victim making the prickly leaves excoriate the lips of her delicate crack in a most cruel manner whilst Lucidora slashes away with the whip on her devoted bottom, gradually cutting and tearing the drawers into fragments.

Poor Haidee, quite exhausted, seems almost dead to the pain, sobbing lower and lower, with occasional sighs of "Ah! Oh! My God, pity me!" The blood slowly trickles down the inside of her thighs and her bottom is a mass of raw, bleeding weals; she gets weaker and weaker; the blows seem to fail in effect; she's impervious to feeling and in spite of all their efforts, she loses consciousness at last.

Sir Charles: "Let her down and apply some of those famous Turkish restorative salts to her nose, that you told me of, Lucidora; let us have some of your Seraglio tales of the harem, or what you may like to call them, whilst she is coming round."

The new assistant is very assiduous in her attentions to the unconscious girl, fanning her face and body all over with a large Oriental fan, covered with Chinese devices of a most voluptuous description whilst Madame, by her directions, applies the Turkish salts, from time to time, to the nostrils, until at last sighs and signs of revival manifest themselves in deep breathing and the victim's hands unwittingly cover and rub the beautiful mount, as if considerable amatory excitement still raged in that part.

"Now," says Lucidora, "is the time to thoroughly awaken her," saying which she puts some of the aromatic salts on her hand and proceeds to rub and tickle the clitoris and tender lips of the poor victim's virgin crack; the effect is so smarting and stimulating that Haidee instantly opens her eyes, exclaiming as she does so: "You devil! Oh! Ah! Let me alone! Oh! Don't excite me so! I can't help what I do!" wriggling and twisting in voluptuous rapture as she lays on the floor, blushing with shame and yet unable to restrain herself.

Sir Charles (laughing): "Ha! Ha! Ha! You have made the lecherous girl show her true character; and yet she pretends to be modest and shocked at the degradation; fie, fie, oh Miss Haidee! Who would have thought of such a mock modest young lady! Now for some tales of the harem."

"This brings to my mind," says Lucidora, "a tale I have heard of a late Sultan, who, being middle-aged and worn out with his amorous exertions in the well-filled Seraglio determines to seek some fresh excitement; everything seems so insipid and blasé to him.

At first he is at a loss how to amuse himself, but one day discussing with his chief eunuch the arrangements and routine of the harem, a circumstance which never gave him a thought before suddenly gave him an idea that he might get both satisfaction and excitement from, viz, that when he came to the throne (he was nephew to the previous Commandeur of the Faithful), he left the Sultana Valide unmolested who in the lifetime of his predecessor had intrigued, in every possible manner, to set aside his succession in favour of her own son, contrary to the usual Osmanli custom. Since which time the baffled Sultaness, a beautiful lady of about thirty, had peevishly shown her hatred of him by keeping in strictest seclusion, only walking by herself, quite unattended, in the most secluded part of the extensive gardens of the Seraglio, at a time when no other ladies of the harem were likely to be about.

The Sultan had heard of the once-famous beauty of this proud lady and was assured by the chief of the eunuchs that she was still surpassing lovely and was suspected of indulging in every variety of voluptuousness with the ladies of her suite in private.

Sultan: "At what hour does she generally take her walk in the garden?"

Chief of the Eunuchs: "About, seven in the morning, your Majesty; she is an early riser and first, goes to the Mosque, then walks in the garden for an hour or more, or sits under a tree reading some exciting French work but retires as soon as the eunuch gardeners are likely to disturb her."

Sultan: "Well, good; keep the gardeners from that part of the grounds tomorrow, I will have a private interview with her Majesty."

Chief of the Eunuchs: "Her Majesty would feel insulted to be addressed in the garden, even by the Sultan. Consider, Sire, her late position and what deference she would expect even from your Majesty yourself."

Sultan: "By the beard of the prophet! I'll bring her to her senses without even telling her who I am. She has never seen me, it will afford infinite satisfaction to witness her haughty proud indignation at a stranger's intrusion on her privacy. But leave me to consider her dignity; all I want is for you to keep all intruders out of the way and be sure to awaken me early enough in the morning."

Next day at an early hour the Sultan is ready for his anticipated excitement; it is a lovely morning in early Spring and he thoroughly enjoys the invigorating soft sea breeze which rustles the leaves of the trees over his head.

Seating himself on the grass behind an oleander thicket close to a pretty little lake so as to command a long vista of one of the principal walks he quietly gives himself up to a reverie between the whiffs of his chibouque: "Ah! to think I have not thought of her before the beautiful haughty Eudoxia. Oh! Allah! What a fine revenge for all she did against me. What a delicious time of day. How curious that although I can scarcely get my poor cock to rise his head at the prettiest of my odalisques one always awakes in the morning with a standing pego. What is the cause of it; perhaps it indicates the proper time of day for voluptuous indulgence. Ah! yes! That must be so, for I always notice how I am, especially if I have indulged in too much Frankish brandy over night; that's our only stimulant. Ah! Allah! Why did the prophet forbid up the glorious wine; spirits were not known then or he would have put a veto on that also. Women, women, nothing but women for good believers. What a man that prophet must have been, and after all nothing else for us in heaven; shall we never be exhausted or cloyed with pleasure there. Ha! Ha! Ha! Of course I'm a true Mussulman, but it takes a big faith to believe all that, or about Iso either. Religion is a manufactured article in all countries, a monopoly not to be interfered with lightly, but no one will know the mystery till after death. How true the saying of Solomon that 'the only real good is to enjoy your life and thank God for it.' There is but one God, whoever is his prophet, we were never intended to make ourselves miserable.

"Ah! Xerxes must have been like myself when he offered such rewards for a new pleasure, he had found himself used up all. Vanity and vexation of spirit. Vanity of vanities, saith the preacher, who had three hundred princesses for wives and seven hundred concubines.

"It was Xerxes who married Esther. Queen Vashti reminds me of the Sultana Valide; how I will humble her and enjoy seeing her humiliated rage, as she finds herself helpless in my power.

"Esther, they say, won the king's heart through the voluptuous instructions imparted to her by Mordecai, all the other virgins only just submitted themselves to the Royal Ravisher, but Esther not only did that but when he was spent with his first efforts played with him, sucked his affair, and after all presented her beautiful bottom to his aroused priapus, which so excited him he was obliged to ravish that also, and finally put the crown on her head, not as the most beautiful of all the virgins, but simply to reward the erotic excitement she had raised by her dalliance.

"Oh, that I had such a nice girl in my harem! They are all duffers.

"Ha! There she comes up the walk," catching a glimpse of the beautiful Sultana coming towards him, all unveiled and book in hand, evidently intent on seating herself under a tree close at hand.

Watching all her actions the Sultan continued to enjoy his smoking and after a little while the lady seated herself on a little mount of grass under a shady tree and proceeded to peruse her book, soon being so absorbed in its contents that she did not perceive his stealthy approach from behind, so that he actually stood at her back, looking over her shoulder and reading the same page as she was feasting upon. The title of the work was "Le Diable au Corps," a most erotic and sensual book, which seemed so to excite her that she sighed and swayed herself about, whilst one hand was quite lost under her clothes and seemed to the Sultan to be very curiously engaged somewhere.

She reads and he reads, she sighs and he sighs, but unnoticed by the beautiful student.

What charms he can see, all down her neck, and the voluptuously rounded bosom, having just under his eyes the dazzling white skin and blue black hair streaming in three long plaits down her back, the lovely delicate hands and plump rounded arms.

How curious it is that anything improper or forbidden has such an exciting effect upon all mankind. Here the Sultan, who feasts unmoved upon the delicious charms of hundreds of lovely girls in the harem, is strangely excited by the beauties so unwittingly exposed to his view.

His manly weapon rises in all its forgotten vigour; the Sultana has thrown back the light shawl which covered her shoulders, so as to leave her neck quite exposed. He frigs himself over his unsuspecting victim, when she suddenly drops backwards at full length, her eyes closed, a sensuous smile of enjoyment upon her lips, her legs rather apart, with one knee bent upwards and the hitherto unseen hand evidently working something under her clothes as she sighs and almost sobs with pleasure, her beautiful legs are quite exposed with nothing on them but delicate slippers on the feet; drawers seem quite wanting in the royal apparel.

Sultans are mortal and however he might have wished to prolong and enjoy the sight it was impossible for him to restrain his own emotions.

The ecstatic moment has arrived. He directs his swollen, excited member downwards and showers a good stream of sperm all over her face, neck and bosom, laughing. "Ha! Ha! Ha! By the prophet you're a wanton woman. What the devil have you got under your clothes?"

Thunderstruck, crimsoning with shame, the Sultana's eyes start open, then she hides her face in her shawl, shrieking: "Ah! Ah! Help! A man! A man!"

The Sultan, giving her a vigorous kick: "You may scream, who's to help you; do you want to expose your own shame or do you really want a man?"

She springs to her feet and attempts to fly but he dexterously catches the tail of her dress and in the endeavours to effect her escape pulls her clothes over her head so that she is quite covered up and her arms helpless whilst every part of her beautiful body, from the waist downwards, is fully exposed.

What a sight meets his gaze; a splendid swelling mount, all covered with long, black, curly hair, extending far over her beautiful belly and some inches down the inside of her thighs, most extraordinary large, round buttocks, quite out of proportion for her size, but so exciting to behold and replete with voluptuous inducements.

Sultana (shrieking): "Ah! Ah! How shameful! Oh! Oh! Let me go or your life will pay the forfeit."

Sultan: "Ha! Ha! You will indeed spare my life lady." Whilst still keeping her head and hands in helpless state he inflicts a furious kick on her bottom, which he repeats again and again, as she begs and cries for mercy, promising everything she can think of to be released. Her bottom is bruised all over and slightly bleeding in places.

Sultana: "Oh! Oh! Oh! Allah! Have mercy. Deliver me from this demon."

Sultan: "Ha! Ha! Cry away to Allah; you ought to be one of the Peers in the prophet's heaven. A wanton woman like you would be properly employed there; what's that instrument I see lying on the grass, dropped from you just now. Tell me this instant what it is or I will murder you."

Sultana: "Oh! Oh! Mercy! It's only a French godemiche."

Sultan: "A godemiche; what's that for? Speak up." Giving another furious kick.

Sultana: "Oh! Oh! We ladies use it to excite ourselves. Oh! If you only knew who I am!"

Sultan: "Indeed, Madame, tell me pray, perhaps I may show you some respect."

Sultana (hopefully): "You little think, for I'm the Sultana Valide; it will be fearful for you if anyone should come and catch you."

Sultan: "Ha! Ha! You wish me to believe that you wanton; now tell me true, are you not one of the lower women of the palace?" Kicking again, this time on her belly, so as to almost make her faint with the shock.

Sultana (shrieking): "Oh! Oh! Mercy! I am indeed the Sultana. Oh! Mercy! Oh!" as kicks follow in quick succession.

Sultan: "So you really want me to believe that, do you?" taking advantage of a cessation of her struggles to secure her to a small tree, with her clothes still over her head, as helpless as before. "Now, you lying woman, I'll teach you to pass yourself off as a Sultana. Here." Placing the godemiche to her cunny.

"I'll give you pleasure; tell me how you feel, if I do it nicely or not, or I'll murder you on the spot. Wait a little, I have got a better idea; you must do it yourself. Feel my knife," said he, again pricking the point twice into her fat bottom and making the blood run freely. "Resist and I kill you; turn round."

So he alters the fastening till she is extended full length on her back, still secured to the little tree, then with his knife cuts a hole through her clothes, so she can just put out one hand and use the godemiche.

"That will do, work away at once, I'm going to make a nice little switch from this prickly shrub to keep you up to your work."

The poor Sultana, nearly dead with fright, does her best to obey.

His rod of prickly twigs cut and scratch her hips and thighs and sometimes the mount, drawing drops of blood at every stroke.

She frantically works her instrument, presenting to his view, as he kneels close in front of her, a most luscious and voluptuous sight, for she is one of those rare women who are splendidly furnished with an enlarged clitoris and prominent, pouting lips to her cunny, which are now plainly seen as they draw out and recede, clinging lasciviously to the working godemiche. Dropping the switch he amuses himself by pinching and nipping her clitoris, and all round the gaping, luscious mouth of her vermilion gap.

His touch seems to electrify her; she screams with

delight.

"Oh, oh, oh! How you make me come, how hot I am. Good heavens! Allah! Allah!" and spends with such profusion that it shoots all over his fingers as the godemiche is still worked vehemently by her nervous hands.

Sultan: "Now withdraw that nasty thing and let me inspect your wanton crack; you're never a modest woman to have behaved as you have; give me that godemiche, I'll put it in my pocket."

Sultana: "Oh pity me! Let me go now! Do have mercy!"

Sultan: "You bitch of a dog, who are you; now confess or you shall be more and more punished."

Sultana: "Oh, oh, mercy! I am indeed the Valide. If this was found out nothing would save me for the Sultan is my enemy!"

Sultan (laughing ironically): "Ha! Ha! You think he would have you thrown into the Bospherous in a sack, do you? How many poor girls have you served so in your time?"

Sultana: "Oh none! I was never cruel or jealous like some of the favourites."

Sultan: "Such lies convince me you are not what you pretend to be; now speak the truth, will you? I might as well tell you I am the Padishah himself. Did he never have you? They say he's been a regular goat in the harem."

Sultana: "You won't believe me; oh! mercy! mercy! I've been a chaste woman all my life."

Sultan (beginning to flog her again with the prickly twigs) "Chaste, chaste, chaste—I should think so after what I have seen," giving scratching switches at every word.

The poor woman kicks about and writhes in agony—her flesh is soon covered with blood which only seems to more excite his fury. She screams wildly for mercy, sobbing for mercy. "Ah! Ah! Oh! Allah! Mercy holy prophet! I shall die! Oh! finish me!"

His excitement is now at the highest. He throws himself on her, exclaiming: "Holy prophet, holy prophet; that puts me in mind of your bottom hole," throwing her legs over his shoulders, he first plunges his bursting instrument into her cunny to well lubricate it, then presents the head to her dark brown fundus. He thrusts furiously and soon gains a partial insertion. "Oh, oh, you'll split me," she screams. "Not there, not there; I never would let the Sultan do that. Oh! Oh! Never! What shame. What filthiness!" She sighs as he pushes on and on, to complete possession, and rests a little after his exertions, but the nervous nippings and contractions of the fundamental canal are too exciting. He spends a stream of his essence into her bowels, which she involuntarily meets with a slight heave of her bottom. Both of them exhausted, remain quite still for some few minutes, affording him infinite pleasure as he causes his dilated instrument to respond to the contracting pulsations of her anus.

Sultan: "Are you finished now, you wanton," withdrawing from her body with a noise something like the drawing of a cork, so tightly is the muscle of her bottom-hole contracted round his still inflamed affair. "Ah! ah! How tightly you hold; haven't you had enough? Ha, ha! I'll take a love token from you, just to remember your pussey when I look at it." So saying he again draws his small knife, which is not very sharp, and proceeds to cut off a good lock of the fine long black curly hair on her cunny. "I must have enough to make a bracelet for my wife; she will little think where it came from," he said, hacking away again and again, causing excruciating pain.

"Oh! Ah! Help, help! Oh, do have mercy! My God!"

she sobs. "I shall never be able to take a bath, my assistants will see it's all gone. Oh, oh, pity me!" She screams, but he cuts on, enjoying her screams and sobbing oh's, till the mouth of her crack looks like a chin unshaved for a fortnight.

"You lying woman, I have made a nice Sultana of your pussey for you, and now I'll really finish you off and let you go."

Sultana: "Holy prophet! Be merciful! Oh, what more misery can you inflict?" sobbing and moaning.

Sultan (stuffing a tuft of grass up her fundus): "That will keep out the cold; it would be a pity for a Sultana to catch cold."

Her legs are wide open, showing the gaping red lips and clitoris of her pussey, all smeared as they are with blood and sperm; then gathering several tufts of grass with the earth hanging to the roots, he proceeds to pelt her cunny with them until one fairly sticks in the entrance. The poor woman is almost unconscious, moaning and sighing, incapable of any effort to save herself.

With a brutal laugh he shoves his toe into her crack, saying: "Now the cold will be kept out there, too." Then unloosing her clothes and allowing her to uncover her face, he enjoys the spectacle of her tearful, pitiable looks as she sobs and moans in her exhausted state. "Ha, ha! A little water will revive you, you wanton Sultana; you'd better pick yourself up and get back to your apartments," said he, making water all over her and even into her gasping mouth.

She chokes, gasps and falls back in a lifeless swoon. This last indignity has finished her; so leaving her to recover as best she could, he retires from the scene. A few days afterwards the Sultan requests an audience of the Sultana Valide as he hears she has been indisposed, and when ushered into her apartment, she receives him unveiled, in consequence of his exalted rank, as her sovereign.

The Sultan (refusing to be seated): "Madame, hearing you were ill I have brought you a present, which I hope may restore your animation a little, especially if you use it vigorously as I have seen you do." And places in her hands a casket of morocco leather, ornamented with gold, which contains her godemiche. "If your Imperial Highness will look, you will see how I have improved it. (He had put a quantity of her own hair on the naked India rubber to make the instrument look more natural.) I have still enough left to make myself a keepsake," said he, inclining his head as he withdrew from her apartment. "Au revoir; I have repaid you for all your former kindness to me."

You may imagine the angry, furious looks of indignant hate which she cast on him as he looked steadily at her enjoying her shame and confusion whilst presenting his present.

Sir Charles and Madame both laugh immoderately at this tale.

"By Jove! Lucidora, I hope you know a few more such stories; it is the best I have ever heard," said the Baronet, looking towards Haidee, whom he had watched all through the narration. "How our chaste, modest Miss has enjoyed it; she looks quite animated again; look at her!"

Haidee is all confusion; her face crimson and eyes flashing with anger, as if she had been the Valide herself.

They lift her up and give her a stimulating cordial, administered in a fizzing, refreshing drink, and the victim allows herself to be fastened to the ladder, which is inclined at a considerable angle; her feet are fastened to the bottom rungs, whilst she is bent forward and her hands fastened within about eighteen inches of her feet, so as to form a forward curve in her body, and present the already lacerated bottom even more conspicuously with the skin tightened by the curvature of her form.

Sir Charles: "What a delicious sight! How tempting! Is it possible to withstand the pleasure of whacking such a posterior?"

Madame: "How beautifully you cut her up, Lucidora; wait a moment Sir Charles, let's see how Adam and Eve's costume will become such a shamefaced, modest young lady; producing and fitting on to her a long elegant wreath of fig leaves made of glazed green paper, fixed on a wire stalk, which contrary to the natural original, was made with numerous short and fine prickly metal thorns, all along the stem which passes round her loins and even between her legs, to join and fasten behind.

Haidee (as she feels the pricks and fears the coming shower of cuts): "Oh! Oh! Oh! Mercy! Oh! Oh! I'll submit; indeed I will. Oh! Madame, intercede for me!"

Sir Charles: "Not yet! Not yet! You've defied and scorned us so long; do you think we will let you off to insult us again!" giving a first preliminary switch with a whalebone rod, made of numerous small fine pieces, fastened together in a handle. "You must be thoroughly subdued; how otherwise can we rely upon your promises? Will you be so obstinate and disrespectful in future? Will you, proud Miss?" All the while he is speaking the whalebone keeps hissing through the air, cutting down on the raw-looking bottom, scattering the green paper leaves about in every direction.

The poor victim screams in the greatest agony, each blow causes the prickly stem to tear and lacerate her more and more; the whalebone is sharp and cuts the delicate skin so that the blood freely trickles down her thighs.

Haidee: "Ah! Ah-r-r-re! Oh! Oh! Mercy! Sir Charles, I'll never dispute your authority again. Oh! indeed, never, never; Oh! Mercy!"

Sir Charles: "Will you—will you—do everything you are ordered in the future, you obstinate girl?"

Haidee: "Oh! Yes! Ah-r-r-re! I could not help it," as in her agony she involuntarily passes a quantity of excrement. (They had administered a powerful aperient in the effervescent drink with the cordial.)

Sir Charles: "The dirty girl! The filthy thing!" cutting away relentlessly, "why now you shall eat it, or I will flog you to death."

Haidee (with horror): "Oh! Oh! Anything; but spare my life! Oh! I shall die if you don't let me down; this position is awful."

Sir Charles is so excited that at this point he wants to enculer the victim, but is restrained by Madame, who makes him strip himself naked and stand before the victim, exhibiting his stiff excited pego; they then unloose Haidee's hands and alter the angle of the ladder so that they may be fastened higher up and give Sir Charles a fair view of her countenance. Lucidora, with a spoon, has gathered some of the excrement into a plate and proceeds to feed the victim.

Madame has provided herself with a fine fresh bunch of nettles, as a whip, so that she may attend to both Sir Charles and Haidee at the same time.

Madame: "Now, Sir Charles, you are so excited. I intend to give you a new voluptuous sensation. Watch carefully and see how our dear Haidee enjoys her supper; she cannot complain, as she provided it herself."

Lucidora, with a small spoon, offers some of the filthy stuff to poor Haidee, as Madame says: "Now, Miss, this is your last humiliation; we will spare you and let you down as soon as you finish it; if you hesitate at all I must remind you with this," flourishing the whip before the poor cowed and exhausted girl.

Haidee, with a gasping effort, opens her mouth; the spoon is inserted, but nature is too powerful; her nausea and disgust are so violent that she vomits and retches till her very stomach seems powerless to do more; exhausted and sinking she gets weaker and weaker, only slightly moaning from time to time; her head droops and she presents a pitiable sight indeed; her face and arms and the front of her body all covered with the vomited excrement and contents of her stomach.

Meanwhile Madame has been whipping Sir Charles' excited instrument with the nettles and now and then waking up his posteriors with a sharp cut of the whip and calling his constant attention to the spectacle presented by poor Haidee.

The nettles strike sharply and the stinging sensation creates such intense excitement, especially when every now and then the bunch is smartly applied to the tender purple head of his swollen member; this combined with the enjoyment of the victim's fearful sufferings, and slowly approaching state of unconsciousness, produce such delicious sensations that at last he shoots forth in ecstasy a torrent of spendings and almost swoons with the delightful thrill which seems nearly to arrest the beatings of his heart.

The victim by this time has really fainted, so with Sir Charles' consent she is carried to her apartment and further torture postponed for the present to allow the principal actor to recover himself.

An Anecdote Conversazione

During the next few days, Sir Charles, Lucidora and Madame have many consultations as to their future proceedings, and finally arrange that the next séance shall be a kind of Anecdote Conversazione, in which the punishments shall be varied as much as possible by calling upon every one present to relate something in turn. It is also decided that Sir Charles may now fairly throw aside all subterfuge with respect to his victims and let them fairly understand that it is for his excitement and amusement he has got them into his power and point out to them that bye and bye they will duly appreciate it themselves.

All are to be assembled except the little Melissa, who is to be kept in reserve for the present.

Every thing being settled, the next evening finds Sir Charles in his chair in the lecture room, dressed in a splendid loose dressing gown, so that he may easily disencumber himself of his clothing when necessary. Madame, in full evening costume stands at his right hand as mistress of the ceremonies whilst Lucidora ushers in the victims, Haidee, Flora, Alice, Veneria, and Sophia, the two latter novices, all smiles and animation, in their blissful ignorance of what is to come; the others very grave and reserved, as if hoping by some means to avoid particular notice. Each one has to pass before the chair with a respectful curtsey, before taking her station as indicated by Madame with a motion of her hand.

The door is locked, and Sir Charles, without further ceremony, addresses them as follows:

"My dear girls:

"Three of you have already experienced the severity with which I can punish even trivial offences; it was then done as a parental duty for your future good; obstinacy always ought to be properly corrected; but there is another kind of chastisement which perhaps neither Alice, Flora nor even Haidee can yet understand; and my object in having you all here this evening is to illustrate to you if possible, the theory of chastisement by which men and women of very sensual temperaments derive from it in various ways the most exquisite enjoyment.

"You, Veneria and Sophia, may not know that I brought you all to this place not to act as a father to you, but to gratify my penchant for humiliating and punishing chaste, modest young ladies who have hitherto never experienced the sense of burning shame, accompanied by violent, excruciating whippings on your bare bottoms or any other part of your naked bodies. Human nature is curious to understand what is torture to some affords infinite pleasure to others. The sight of a victim's blood has a most stimulating effect upon nerves.

"Peter the Great once took upon himself the task of executioner and cut off with his own hands the heads of some scores of his Strelitz Guards and found such pleasurable excitement in the exercise that he desisted only when fairly exhausted and unable any longer to wield his bloody weapon.

"One of his successors, the Empress Catherine, so noted for her sensuality and debauchery before indulging with her favourites in amorous and voluptuous dalliance had resort to tortures of various kinds for the purpose of heating her blood to the necessary pitch of erotic excitement. Upon one occasion she had compelled a young princess of a noble Russian house to marry one of her favourite paramours, a man of a most brutal temperament and originally nothing but a peasant. This ill-assorted marriage, as you may assume, produced nothing but misery for the poor girl, who after enduring every kind of indignity and violence at the hands of her cruel husband, appealed to the Empress for redress.

"Catherine made her fully relate all she had suffered, then laughing ironically, ordered her attendants to strip the poor princess perfectly naked, when, unable to perceive any marks of the alleged ill usage, she orders one of her attendants to take the victim on her back, in the most approved style, whilst the Empress herself, with a small leather knout, inflicted dreadful punishment, each blow cutting out pieces of the victim's flesh and making the blood run in a stream, crying:

"'There, there—does he whip you anything like that; or do I hurt you as much as your husband! Why, you haven't a bruise on you, you lying little wife; don't you know that every Russian husband shows his love by whipping or beating his wife and the wives are not happy if their husbands don't thrash them well and frequently? There, there—go home; the more he beats you the more certain you may be of his love.'

"Another time a lovely girl not much over twelve years of age threw herself at the Empress' feet, imploring pardon for her father, who had just been sentenced to death for some political offence.

"The Empress asked her if she was willing to suffer anything for her parent, and if she was certain she could bear a good whipping with fortitude, 'for if you scream for mercy your father will lose his life.'

"The poor girl assured her Majesty she would die to save her father; so the cruel, voluptuous woman, to feed her own sensuality, made the poor girl undergo most frightful tortures in her presence; she was first beaten with thin flat boards on her bare bottom. This was very painful, but produced no visible marks, except a beautiful red flush all over the surface, then the little victim was stripped quite naked, laid flat on the face and flogged all over with a scourge of small cords (they seldom used such a mild instrument as the birch rod in Russia); her tender flesh was cut and bleeding from shoulders to thighs, the poor girl all the while resolutely restraining her screams, and only moaning fainter and fainter as she gets exhausted, to the great annoyance of the infernal Empress, who had no wish to grant her father's pardon, but desired to gratify her own passion for cruelty, and also by compelling the victim to scream for mercy to avoid the promised clemency to her parent.

"At last the sight of the blood and writhing, moaning agony of the sufferer so infuriated this human tigress that she seized a heavy driving whip, and ordering the victim to be turned over on her sore back, she lashed the poor little thing furiously across her face and bosom, every cut breaking the skin, and covering her with blood and bruises. This indeed brought excruciating cries of agony, but none for mercy. She, with infinite cruelty continued to slash her all over, across the tender belly, thighs and legs; no part was left unscathed, and finally in her rage beat the victim in a most brutal manner with the handle of the whip, till she was supposed to be dead.

"This evening we have invited you here, Veneria and Sophia, to begin your castigatory education, the others have gone through their first course; it won't be so bad for them. Ha! Ha! You may turn pale and crimson and look down in confusion; it's the sight of your distress that affords us such pleasure; the more you scream, cry or show signs of misery the more delightfully exciting it is to us. The rest of the company will be called on to tell some tale or anecdote of a flagellatory nature, to enliven the proceedings, so Haidee, Flora and Alice, just refresh your memories to save your posteriors and remember the more racy you make the stories, the better for yourselves."

Madame: "We will begin with Haidee, she must put the others through the first course. Now Haidee, just take this birch," handing an elegantly tied light bunch of twigs. "Undress yourself, the same as we did you the other evening; first the outer silk dress, then petticoats; pause awhile to let us compare all your beauties, legs, feet, bosoms, etc., touch any of them up smartly who do not obey. You know how to obey; make the others do the same or I shall give you a smart reminder."

Haidee (throwing off her dress): "Now Flora, now Veneria, come, come Sophia," swishing the birch towards the frightened girls.

Madame (sharply): "Do your duty; no tenderness!"

Haidee (giving Flora a smart stroke over her shoulders): "You ought to be quicker, and you too, Alice!" touching her up.

The two novices are all confusion; their faces pale and blush with extraordinary emotion; Sophia is in tears.

"Oh! Oh! Haidee, how can you strip us so before every one?"

Haidee (giving her a smart cut on her bare arm which leaves a reddish mark): "Silence Miss, how dare you! Now, all face Sir Charles and lift your petticoats above your knees; up—up higher, Sophia! Now, Veneria, look up, no shamefacedness,"—giving her a smart cut on the shoulder as a reminder.

Sophia and Veneria (together): "Oh, oh! Haidee, how shameful!"

Haidee: "Now, Sir Charles," lifting her own petticoats, and blushing for shame at the part she is obliged to act, "you have five pairs of beautiful legs to compare and admire; do we please you; shall we lift our clothes higher?"

Sir Charles, going from one to the other, handles and examines all their legs, and even passes his hand up their drawers, to pinch and feel the firm flesh of their thighs. He pays particular attention to Veneria and Sophia, who are all burning blushes at his libidinous pinches; they drop their clothes and spring away from his touch with indignant ejaculations, but are speedily brought into the rank again by Madame and Lucidora, who push them forward into their places, and pinch and slap their bottoms as they lift their clothes from behind.

They scream and sob with mortification at this forced degradation.

"Oh! Oh! Oh! How nasty! How awful! Oh! Oh! Take us away!"

Madame (screaming at the loudest): "Now Haidee, Haidee, keep the girls to their work. Up with all your clothes to your waists; Sir Charles, she is remiss in her duty; we shall have to make her an example to the younger ones."

Sir Charles: "Steadily, steadily; I can see she's useless to keep the others in order; do you, Madame, take them in hand, all five in a row; how delicious the sight will be."

Madame, slashing all along the line, gives Haidee a dreadful cut across the face with the lady's whip. Always such an effectual instrument, the blow makes her lips swollen and leaves a long red mark from mouth to ear; the poor girl's eyes are full of tears and she bites her lips with rage and humiliation.

"Up, up with your clothes right under your arms," thunders Madame, slashing Veneria and Sophia unmercifully over their bare shoulders, raising weals at every cut. Flora and Alice also come in for their share, and all four cry out in anguish.

"Yes, Madame, we will! We will! Oh! Oh! Give us time to do it!"

"Now, girls," as Lucidora, from behind, has pinned up every victim's skirts, "attention! Hands by your side!"

Sir Charles: "Ha! Ha! Make them go through their drill like recruits."

Madame: "Now Veneria, open your drawers a little in front and ask Sir Charles if he would like to have a peep at your pussey. Tell him to feel how nice and soft it is; quick—quick, Miss Shameface!" slashing her on her hands and almost making the poor girl jump with pain. "Do you hear what I say? Speak up plainly."

Veneria: "Ah! Ah! Ah-r-r-re! My hands are so hurt. Oh! Mercy! It's impossible!"

Madame (slashing her across her head and shoulders): "Make haste or you shall be cut to pieces; do as you are bid, this instant."

Veneria: "Mercy, mercy! Sir Charles—do—do—do—do you wish to see me? Oh oh! My nice little pussey, it's so soft. Oh! Oh! May I show it to you?" The last few words are spoken in spasmodic gasps as she convulsively opens her drawers in front, and exposes the beautiful, dark silky moss of her finely covered mount.

Madame has been all the while cutting her about with merciless blows of the whip, and the poor girl is beside herself with pain and same.

Sir Charles kneels down in front of her, tickling and playing with the lips of her crack, whilst Madame makes the poor girl stammeringly tell him, (dictating word for word):

"Oh, how nice! How it makes me love you, Sir Charles. Don't you think mine is a very pretty little cunny?"

Then he examines and feels all the others in the same way.

Poor little Sophia is ready to faint with pain and shame, whilst Alice, Flora and Haidee evince their degradation and humiliation by hysterical sobbing, sighing and tears, till at last the latter is unable to restrain her indignation any longer and shrieks out frantically: "Oh! Oh! Ah! Shameful; kill me at once and spare me the sight of my poor sisters' horrible treatment. Take me and finish me off at once; work your fiendish will on me, but spare them the sight of it. Ah! Ah! My God! Mercy! Deliver me from these inhuman demons!" as Madame slashes her brutally across the face and mouth to silence her.

Sir Charles: "Tie her up! Tie her up!" the sight of her bleeding features and resolute indignation beginning to excite him more and more.

Madame and Lucidora speedily secure the unresisting victim to the ladder, with her clothes well pinned up, her hands tied high above her head, so that she can only just touch the ground with the tips of her toes and her ankles being also secured she is prevented from stepping on the rungs of the ladder to ease the painful position; then slightly opening her drawers behind to partly expose the voluptuous cheeks of her bottom, she is left for the present, a sacrifice ready to be offered at any moment.

Madame: "There, young ladies, see how we truss you up? Mind it isn't head downwards when your turns come; now right about face."

They turn sideways to Sir Charles, giving him a profile view of their indignant, blushing faces, crimson with shame and furrowed with tears. "Now again quite around; open your drawers behind and let Sir Charles see the beauties of your posteriors. Pull up your chemise and bow forward so as to give a good view.

One—two—three—four" she says, slashing each bent bottom in turn, as if to count them for Sir Charles. "One—two—three—four; how nicely I can do the musical scales, from treble to soprano," making each one cry out: "Oh! Ah! Ah! Ah!" in quick succession, which with the red weals and blushing bottoms, afford Sir Charles and Madame exquisite pleasure.

Sir Charles: "Haidee is to have twenty-four good strokes of the birch, whilst Flora shall take Sophia, and Veneria Alice across their knees, open their drawers behind, and keep time with you, Madame, giving hearty slaps on the bottom at each stroke of your rod."

Madame (selecting a fine large bunch of birch, the handle covered with blue velvet and ornamented with magenta-coloured ribbons): "This is a fine swish-tail; there won't be much of her drawers left when I've done. Now then girls; Lucidora take the whip and see that they do their duty by the little ones."

Sophia: "'Oh! Flora, dear, don't be so cruel!"

Alice: "Poor Sophia, we must submit; they must do it or be fearfully beaten."

Veneria (kissing Alice's bottom most lovingly): "Oh! Oh! Indeed I would rather you did it to me, poor Alice, forgive me dear for what we are compelled to do."

Lucidora: "Now be ready; Madame is going to begin with Haidee."

Madame (to her victim): "You want me to make you an example don't you? Sir Charles have you noticed her scornful looks; she must be made to look different from that; her punishment the other day has had very little effect. Now! One—two—three!" Whack! Slap! Slap! Whack! Slap! Slap! Whack—Slap! Slap! "Harder you girls; your slaps have no sound in them. Lucidora, look after them, pray."

Each blow of the birch falls with telling effect on the

well-stretched bottom of poor Haidee, cutting and fraying the drawers and raising great blushing weals across her buttocks in every direction; she is too extended to writhe but shrieks and cries out in great agony:

"Oh! Oh! Ah-r-r-re! This is worse and worse. My God! What will they do next! Oh! Oh! Kill me! Save the poor children!"

Lucidora meanwhile is busy with her whip, compelling Flora and Veneria to do their duty, scoring their shoulders with weals, and in a few strokes they are brought to slap heavily, keeping proper time, as Madame uses her rod.

The little victims writhe and wriggle as their bottoms smart and tingle at every slap, turning the cheeks of their posteriors to beautiful blushing surfaces.

Sir Charles is in ecstasies; the sight of so many bottoms under punishment at once, the agony and distress of Veneria, the perfect chorus of Ah's, Oh's, sighs, sobs and hysterical crying make such music to his ears, that hardly knowing himself to have arrived at such a climax, he spends under his dressing gown, exclaiming: "Ah, delightful! Draw the blood, Madame; let me see the real carmine."

Madame continues to thrash in earnest and at the twentieth stroke the drawers are all in rags, tattered, torn and bloodstained from the slowly trickling streams which ooze from the broken weals; in fact poor Haidee is in a most deplorable state; her head hangs back almost lifeless, the eyes are closed, with a slight blood-stained foam on her lips, her faint moans are scarcely audible; the victims, in spite of their own agonizing distress, seem almost speechless with terror at the sight; their starting eyes and awestruck faces fully attest the horrible fear they are in, as well as pity for the sufferer.

Sir Charles: "Let her down quickly, the extraordinary tension of the position is killing her; she must
not go yet; we've got a different idea to carry out first."

His intercession is too late to prevent the
approaching swoon, and when let down she lies in an
unconscious heap on the floor. They all cluster round
her the other victims shedding tears, and pitying poor
dear Haidee; they chafe and rub her hands, use the
restorative salts, etc., but for some time without effect;
they give her a strong cordial in the same effervescing
drink as before, and laying her head in a pillow, leave
her to come round by herself, whilst Madame is to
relate some of her experiences.

"I will tell you," said Madame, "about an English
lady and her daughter. The account was given to me
by a French gentleman, who used a few years ago to
visit my house in Paris; he was a very handsome,
noble and wealthy man and had the good fortune at a
ball to fall in love with the lady; the result was that she
became desperately enamoured of him and determined
in her mind that he should marry her. They enjoyed a
most voluptuous liaison for some weeks, but Madame,
just as she already felt assured of her conquest, was
chagrined to find that her daughter of seventeen had
unwillingly taken her place in the heart of her
paramour. Filled with rage and jealousy, she suddenly
left Paris and secluded herself with her daughter in a
lonely chateau, high up on one of the spurs of the
French Pyrenees and having arranged everything to
her satisfaction sends an intimation of her
whereabouts to the Count of Bonvit assuring him that
if he will do her the pleasure of a short visit she will
initiate him into a new mode of voluptuous excitement.

M. de Bonvit has been too much a man of the world
and too surfeited with pleasure to fail in availing
himself of such a chance especially as he hoped to find

there the darling girl who was just then the loadstone of his existence. (He had had a good many such loadstones before.)

As soon as he arrives, Mrs. Amor (that was her name) receives him alone in her boudoir.

"Ah! Monsieur le Comte," she says, "I am so glad and happy you are come, as here I can say to you without fear, what perhaps you would only have treated with scornful laughter in Paris; but here (producing a small revolver from her bosom), I am master of the situation. Promise to love and marry me and I will make your happy; I know you love my daughter and have resolved to sacrifice her to my jealousy; listen, hold! not a word of objection; you would always love her better than me. You shall enjoy and outrage her in my presence when we have sufficiently tortured and humiliated her. Ah! Ha! You little thought I have read de Sade's work. How I have gloated over the scenes of cruelty; much as I have loved my dear Julie, I have now an implacable thirst for revenge; when she is gone you will love me, as you ought, but never while she lives. The thought is maddening; she must be tortured and humiliated to the death. It will give most blissful erotic excitement to us. Do you agree? Yes, or no! Life or death!" Presenting the revolver with starting eyes and furious determination, "She shall not live to be yours!"

De Bonvit, a man of high courage, had often faced his adversary's pistol in duels, but to stand unarmed before a furious woman was a different passage of arms altogether; his love for Julia was indeed strong, but on the other hand he felt assured the female demon before him would never suffer her to live; then also was he not promised possession and every kind of sensual gratification, so that losing his own life would not only entail death of his darling, but loss of voluptuous enjoyment to himself; besides the picture of erotic excitement to be gained by carrying out the mother's intentions had exercised a certain kind of fascination on one who had long secretly wished for an opportunity to test the theories of excitement and exquisite pleasure to be derived from such unnatural cruelties.

He gave the required promise, on his honour as a gentleman, and they passed a delicious evening in voluptuous enjoyment.

He is not permitted to see the beautiful Julia till the next evening, when she is summoned to attend a conference with her mother and Monsieur le Comte. The apartment where they are seated is furnished with a long, low table not more than eighteen inches from the ground; it is nine feet long and four and a half feet wide, covered with red baize cloth and a strong leather ring at each corner furnished with pendant silken cords; the walls are draped with black and yellow curtains all round.

Mrs. Amor: "My dear Julia, M. de Bonvit has honoured us with a flying visit from Paris, on a matter of great importance to yourself. (Julia blushes crimson and casts down her eyes). Don't be shamefaced, turn the key in the lock and bring it to me, then we will discuss cette affaire de coeur."

Julia, in blushing confusion, brings the key to her mother and throws herself on her mamma's neck, sobbing: "Oh, Mother! Mother! It is so unexpected!"

De Bonvit: "Ah! Mademoiselle is so unused to these things; is it not true Madame, that your daughter has only just returned from a select school!"

Mother: "Quite true; she has been in an English school: Our girls are brought up with such mock-modesty they really know nothing. Julia, Monsieur has done you the honour to propose for your hand, but as is usual with Frenchmen desires to assure himself of the reality of your virgin charms in my presence."

Julia (blushing in greatest confusion): "Oh! Oh! Mamma! What do you mean? Surely not to expose myself!"

Mother: "It's quite customary, my dear, in such cases and I am sure you love him, do you not?"

Julia: "Oh Mother! I can never consent to such indelicacy!"

Mother: "Fie! Fie! It is for your future happiness; indeed I must insist upon it. The French are quite right; who would like to marry a girl with bow legs, or some other deformity; stand on the table, my dear, it's nothing at all, nothing; come do it at once; don't waste any more time."

Count: "Allow me, Mademoiselle; this is nothing if done with politeness and delicacy; you are to be my wife dearest; do you think I would insult you?" assisting her on to the table.

Mother: "Now we must first inspect your legs. Draw up your skirts to your knees."

Julia: "Will that do?" raising her dress halfway up her calves.

Mother: "No; don't make me angry; you know how I can punish with the birch although you may think yourself too big for that. I shan't hesitate to let Monsieur have a lesson in domestic discipline if you drive me to it."

Count: "A little higher, Mademoiselle Julia. What beautiful calves!" feeling and stroking her legs.

Mother: "Quite up, above your knees; higher, higher. Julia do you hear?"

Julia: "Oh! Mama dear, how indelicate!" blushing crimson as she pulls up her skirts and drawers to the middle of her thighs.

Count (passing his hand up her drawers and feeling

the firm velvety flesh): "Mademoiselle you have the limbs of an angel; oh how the touch fires my blood!"

Here Julia suddenly lets down her clothes in affright at his increasing boldness, blushing and crimson with confusion. "Oh! No! Never! Never! For shame, Monsieur!"

Mother (in a rage): "How dare you Miss? Obey me this instant or I shall make you," giving her a sound box on the ears, making the poor girl in still greater confusion and bringing the tears into her eyes.

Julia: "Oh, oh! Pity me! Don't compel me to do such things. Oh! Monsieur! Monsieur! Intercede for me!"

Count: "Certainly, ma chere Mademoiselle, but I only want to inspect your charms; it is the same as if we were already married and your mother is present. It is really essentially necessary for you to do all your mother requires."

Mother: "Yes, and I'll spank her well if she is not obedient; I've no patience to be disobeyed by my own daughter. Now, Miss, lift up your clothes as high as before and turn your back to us, so Monsieur can see your calves."

Julia is too frightened not to obey and the Count feels and pinches and pats her calves and thighs whilst he continually apologizes for the necessity of being sure she is quite sound in every respect, and hopes she does not mind it.

Mrs. Amor now makes Julia hold up her clothes, close under her arms, and stepping on the table, secures the skirts of her daughter well over her shoulders, then ordering her sternly, compels the blushing and humiliated girl to open her own drawers behind.

Mother: "Look! Look! Count. What beautiful white, firm buttocks; but I must make them another tint or she will get obstinate." Then she gives Julia two or three loud sounding smacks with her hand, suffusing the cheeks of her bottom with a fine rosy tint. "Ha! Ha! Count," she laughs, "one or two more will improve her docility;" smack, smack, smack, each harder than the other, making the poor girl's bottom smart and tingle with pain. Julia screams: "Oh! Oh! Mother! Mamma! Oh! Have mercy! I shan't be able to sit down for ever so long."

Count: "Poor Mademoiselle, how I pity you; how delicious is the sight of your rosy coloured bottom."

Mother: "It's done for her good, she won't want to sit down for some time yet."

Julia, her face furrowed with tears and turning down her eyes for shame, sighs at the humiliation. "Oh! Oh! Let me go now, pray; you cannot want to see more."

Count (taking her hand lovingly and pressing it to his lips): "Dear Julia, we are only just beginning; it won't hurt you to show me your front, will it?" looking aside with delight at Mrs. Amor.

Mother: "Now kiss me and thank me for correcting you; my other daughter that is married always had to kiss the rod and thank me."

Julia: "Yes, yes, Mamma, you always do it in love," kissing her.

Mother: "Mind I am not obliged to be more severe; turn round and let down your drawers for the Count to examine your front."

Julia's hands tremble and shake, she seems instinctively to know she is to go through some terrible ordeal; with considerable hesitation her hands partly open her drawers, but two or three more lively spanks from behind make her drop them, suddenly, so as to leave all fully exposed, the beautiful full, rounded buttocks, plump, straight thighs and above all a delicious looking mons veneris, covered with soft curly brown hair.

Count: "What heavenly beauties! Permit me dear Julia," parting the soft curly hair with his fingers. She resolutely keeps her eyes closed and is fearfully agitated with shame and confusion. "Ah! Ah! I feel the little rogue," tickling her small clitoris and playing with her, till in spite of herself she gives down her first maiden spend and plentifully bedews his busy fingers. "See, see, Madame," he says to Mrs. Amor, "what a loving girl! How delicious!" putting his fingers in his mouth.

"Now, Mademoiselle Julia, I hope you love me a little. I am going to make you love me still more even if it hurts you a little; be assured it pains me as much as it does you; now put up your drawers and stand stooping forward as if you were bowing to your mother so as to make them fit tightly across your beautiful bottom."

Julia, stooping as requested, but seeing him handling a fine long birch rod, made of a few thin twigs elegantly tied up with blue and red silk ribbons, exclaims: "Oh! Mother! Mother! My God! What is he going to do now? Oh! Oh! Save me, Mother," jumping off the table and running to the further end of the apartment.

Mother: "My dear Count, how could you expect she would stand still to be birched; she must be secured properly; see, this table is as good as a ladder; it has a mechanical contrivance so it can be inclined at any angle and the culprit properly secured to the rings."

Here, each taking an arm, Julia is brought back to the table, in terrible horror of what is going to happen, begging and praying them to have pity. She is quite ready to marry Monsieur, etc., but "Spare me! Oh! Spare me!" she cries, "how can you be so cruel?"

They compel her to divest herself of every thing,

except drawers and chemise; she is made to fix open her drawers behind and tuck up her tail so as to expose as much as possible of her poor downed rump; then they stretch her face-downwards on the table, securing her feet and hands by the silken cords to the rings at the four corners.

Count: "Madame, shall I allow her much freedom of motion; what is your opinion as to distending the victim, or securing her hands?"

Mother: "Her hands must be drawn up as tightly as possible; it increases the pleasure to be derived if she has most of her weight on her arms."

Count: "It is a new sensation to me; these positions are all delightful. Do you allow her to scream, or is she to be gagged with a pocket handkerchief?" tightening her hands as he speaks, whilst Mrs. Armor, turning the handle of a screw, gradually elevates one end of the table till poor Julia is regularly spread-eagled, hanging by her arms from the two top rings, and her feet just touching the floor are loosely secured to the other rings at the lower end of the table.

Mother: "Oh! Let her scream, by all means; it adds music to excitement, and her feet ought to be a little more tightly secured. She has too much freedom, and only just let her toes support her. Now, Count, are you ready? She's all anxiety to feel your loving switches"— laughing ironically at the poor, piteous-looking Julia, who is bathed in tears and trembling in anticipation of her torture; the tension of her limbs and the strain on her wrists already drawing suppressed sighs and moans from her.

Count: "Poor Julia, how I pity you; does that hurt you?" giving a smart little switch to her bottom.

Julia: "Oh! Oh! Have mercy! My wrists are breaking! I can't move! My great toes will be broken! Ah! Oh! How you cut; it's like a knife slashing me every time you strike! Oh! Oh! Mercy! Mother!" as the Frenchman gradually increases the force of his blows. The thin birch twigs raise long, narrow, red looking weals in every direction across her loins and bottom, raising the rosy hue of the flesh to a deeper red blush.

Count: "Poor girl! Dear Julia, don't you feel to love me more and more now? How it warms my blood! You don't imagine how painful it is to me," (darting looks of fiery excitement towards Mrs. Armor who is seated in a chair close to the victim, with one hand under her clothes, and enjoying every convulsive twitching of her daughter's countenance and drinking in all her cries as if they were the sweetest music to her ears).

Mother: "Cry away, my girl; there's a good Julia; it will ease you, my dear, and delight us to hear it; louder; scream louder, dear, you will feel the benefit of it, it will keep your spirits up."

Count: "Ah! Madame! I am sure you do indeed feel for her; Mademoiselle, does that hurt you more?" cutting up under the crack of her bottom, so as to swish the lips of her cunny.

Julia: "Oh! Oh! Awful! Horrible! You're cutting me to bits! Oh! Mercy! Mercy!" Swish—swish—swish, the birch continues to cut the victim's buttocks in between and across her thighs, causing the blood to trickle slowly down her legs. The drawers are reduced to bloodstained rags, whilst poor Julia, in her agony, sobs hysterically for mercy, appealing to her mother and the Count, who are both more and more excited as the poor girl gets weaker and weaker, Mrs. Amor pulling up her clothes and frigging herself desperately in sight of her distressed and horrified daughter, whilst Monsieur, finding her too engrossed in her own sensuality to render him any assistance, throws away the stump of the untied birch, quickly turns the table down to a level, and releasing the victim's feet, makes her kneel on her hands and knees (little thinking of what is to some next). He lets down his trousers and bringing out his excited, bursting priapus, at once throws himself upon her bleeding, lacerated bottom, which he kisses with rapture as he licks the blood off the oozing weals and excites himself to the highest pitch of erotic madness; his fingers search out and part the glowing lips of her wounded slit; they enter and prepare the way for a more important member; he feels the throbbing heat and excited contractions which his touch arouse in those delicate parts, and having well wetted with saliva the head of his affair, he surprises the almost fainting girl by his vigorous assault.

She is so small made that he makes very little progress at first, for the victim instinctively shrinks from his thrusts, which hurt her so much and quite awaken her from her painful lethargy; she shrieks and struggles to avoid this last degradation. "Ah! Ah-r-r-re! You shan't; I'll die first! You horrible man! Oh Mother! Oh! Oh! Spare me! He's killing me! Oh!"

Her cries of pain afford him infinite satisfaction and only add to his furious lust; he clings tightly round her waist and succeeds in partially lodging the head of his instrument just within the lips of her vagina when the victim flattens herself down on the table and baffles his efforts to penetrate further; but he holds her tight and keeps his place, although such a trifling advantage, putting his hands round in front and pinching and nipping her mount to make her heave up her bottom again; but just as all his efforts are likely to fail, the mother comes to his assistance, and getting a large bunch of holly under Julia's belly, forces her to kneel up again, with renewed screams of pain.

Mother: "Now, Monsieur, is your chance; force your entrance quickly; her screams are delightful. How do you like holly, my dear?" to poor Julia.

Julia: "Oh! Oh! What hellish cruelty! Oh! Mother! Mother! Are you too turned into a devil? Oh! Oh! Ah! Kill me at once! He is rending his way into me!" as Monsieur, with redoubled energy, shoves and shoves, till his great pego tears through every virgin obstacle and is fully inserted right up to his testicles. She gives an awful shriek of agony, renewed again and again at each exquisitely excruciating thrust, and when at last the soothing effect of his spendings somewhat ease the painful friction, and he sinks upon her in the lethargy of voluptuous rapture, she is more dead than alive and quite unaware that his instrument is enraptured by the palpitations, contractions and delicious nippings, as she lies vanquished, torn, stretched and bleeding—completely at his mercy.

He moves again, gently at first, trying to arouse in her some of the delightful sensations he has himself enjoyed, then faster, as he feels her unvoluntarily respond to the now soothing motion. Her mother has dropped the holly and is now frigging her daughter with her fingers, and this so excites the Count that he again spends a perfect torrent of his essence into the now enraptured womb of his victim.

Count: "Oh! Oh! How delicious! I feel my life flowing from me into her inmost vitals; how strange I should have been so tremendously excited; it is all caused by the resistance of my dear Julia and the knowledge of her pain and humiliation which she must have felt so. But, see, see, your daughter has fainted; it has been too much for her! how deliciously her tight little cunt contracts and throbs!"

Mother: "I'll soon revive her," applying some powerful pungent salts to Julia's nostrils. "Keep your place till she revives; make your concern throb inside of her, it will all help to bring her round and will excite such pleasurable feelings that she will not be able to restrain them."

The Count does as he is directed, and presently poor Julia, whose tight-fitting sheath is now quite relaxed by the excessive lubrication of Monsieur's spendings, begins to recover, and instead of the previous excruciating pains, feels now nothing but a most voluptuous warmth and pleasurable titillations, only half conscious, she scarcely knows what she is doing or where she is. She wiggles and writhes as the motion seems to alleviate the hot, smarting sensations of her poor bruised posteriors. The Count slowly responds to her movements for fear of awakening her too much, and gradually excites her to a most luscious reciprocation of his motions, and they finally both spend together in an agony of blissful enjoyment.

He presently withdraws, after remaining quietly within her for a few minutes and Julia begins to slowly comprehend the disgusting process which she has so apparently enjoyed.

Mother (laughing ironically): "Fie! Fie! Miss Julia; I did not think you were so rude! I know something else you would like—isn't that nice?" wetting her fingers in her own spendings and putting them into Julia's mouth, who is scarlet with shame and indignation. "What, you don't like it? Ha! Ha! You like somebody else's juice better than mine, to judge by the way you wiggled your bottom as he shot it into you; well you shall taste that, if you prefer it," taking a small tea spoon and carefully scraping some of the blood and sperm which oozed from her glistening slit. "Now, Miss, take this in your mouth or I will cut you to pieces."

Julia, almost ready to vomit with nausea at the disgusting stuff is yet obliged to lick the spoon quite clean. Then they take some champagne and give her a little to wash it down and revive her courage after which she has to put on a new pair of drawers and her feet are again secured to the rings of the table, which they now elevate from the other end, so as to suspend her head downwards.

Mrs. Amor: "Now it is my turn—I am going to complete my revenge. You, Count, have had what I promised you, but I am going to excite you yet once more," saying which she takes up the bunch of holly and begins to thrash the poor victim on her previously lacerated bum and especially between her legs, which are so well distended as to fully expose the red vermilion lips of the recently deflowered slit.

Poor Julia shrieks in agony.

"Oh! Oh! Mother! Oh! Mercy! Mercy! How cruel!" She is too distended to struggle and soon nothing can be heard, whilst the inhuman mother, (laughing and jeering her all the while) makes the Count hold open the cheeks of her bottom so that the holly may scratch and prick all round the little brown bottom hole, making the blood slowly trickle down, both over her back and her snow-white belly at the same time, as the inside of her thighs have been equally pricked and scratched all over.

Count: "How she must suffer! Poor thing! Yet my blood boils with pleasurable emotions, so voluptuous, so delicious; the sight of her beautiful blood excites me more every moment; no earthly love could make me spare her; how delightful to witness her tear-stained, blushing face and notice all the writhings and contractions of her beautiful body."

Mother: "Ah! No one can tell the delicious voluptuousness of my feelings; the very fact of her being my own daughter enhances my sensations ten fold."

Count: "I must help in the flagellation; each blow on

the victim seems to give me an electric thrill as it touches her; stand clear; your torture with the holly is horrible, but is too slow; I will soon cut her drawers off with this whip," flourishing a powerful hunting whip, well tipped with knotted cord; "get out of my way or I shall hit you."

The mother is already tired; she sinks into a chair to gloat over the scene as the Count slashes poor Julia up and down her thighs and buttocks, raising great bleeding weals at every stroke. The victim is now too weak to cry out; her senses seem dulled to pain, her head hangs almost lifeless, with dishevelled hair trailing on the floor. Very faint moans are the only signs that she is still alive; the blood now runs in streams down her back, neck and head, clotting the beautiful brown hair and dripping to the floor. Still the Frenchman, who is no longer conscious of what he is doing, cuts away, slashing round her ribs, on her lovely neck and shoulders, blows, any one of which seem sufficient to kill a delicate girl, till at last he grows dizzy with the excitement, his very life seems to shoot from him as he spends all over the back of the bleeding victim and falls senseless to the ground.

Next morning he awakes to find himself comfortably reposing in the arms of Mrs. Amor and never more sets eyes on the charming Julia, or knew whether she died under his hands or not, but he assured me that none but those who have experienced such heavenly, blissful emotions can possibly understand his voluptuous enjoyment at that scene of martyrdom.

Thus ending, Madame now turns her attention to the business of the evening, once more asking Sir Charles "who is to tell the next tale?"

Sir Charles: "Flora will be the next called upon, but we will first finish Haidee's punishment. Tie her hands to the ladder, level with her face." Madame and

Lucidora soon fasten up the victim once more, then, Sir Charles, taking the cat-o-nine tails, "now, Miss Obstinate, you are to step up one rung of the ladder at each cut, and mind, not two steps at a time, or you will catch it extra hot; now then—one—two—three—four—five," cutting her severely at each word, across her legs, tearing her silk stockings, and drawing blood at every stroke.

Poor Haidee screams at her loudest: "Oh! Oh! My legs! Oh! Will you never have pity! Oh! Let me die in mercy!"

Sir Charles: "Now halt; you are nearly bent out double; when I cut you across your bottom, you must slip your body through the rungs of the ladder and hang out on the other side."

The victim here presents a most interesting object to the spectators, her body almost bent double, her feet now resting only a little below her hands, all her muscles fully displayed and extended, her beautiful bosom drawn tightly forward by the tension of her arms, with her knees and thighs nearly parallel to her lovely belly; the skin of the rump so tightened as to cause a renewed oozing of blood from the broken weals, her pouting slit, with beautiful glossy black hair shading the deliciously luscious red lips is also plainly visible underneath.

Sir Charles: "What a sight for an Epicurean! Now then, through you go!" giving a tremendous cut.

Haidee: "Oh! Oh! Oh! Sir Charles! I shall break my back! Oh! kill me at once in mercy!" slipping forward, but resting her bottom on the rung of the ladder.

Sir Charles: "That won't do; you must slip quite through. Go on, go on, will you!" slashing her bottom cruelly, making the blood spurt in streams and staining the "cat" at every stroke, till the poor victim seems almost to be shoved through by the force of his blows and hangs in a most painful, back-breaking position on one of the rungs of the ladder, with all her weight on her wrists.

Madame (giving each of the girls a pair of pincers): "Now mind, you do as you are ordered; you are to pluck out the hairs of her cunny, taking as few as possible at a time; all four of you are to help, and Lucidora and myself will see you do your duty," flourishing her sharp, cutting whip in their faces.

Thus threatened, Flora, Alice, Veneria and Sophia are made to slowly pluck poor Haidee's mount. Madame and her assistant constantly slashing with their whips to keep them up to their work and every now and then pointing out any little hairs they may have omitted to pluck out, even to the little thin down round her bottom hole. The victim is in dreadful agony, her painful position and the excruciating plucking preventing her from fainting outright. She sighs and sobs and adds to the excitement of her tormentors by kicking down two of the unwilling operators, who are well lashed for their carelessness in allowing her to do it; but the exertion is too much for poor Haidee, her legs hang helpless and she has evidently more injured herself than any one else.

Sir Charles (lighting a candle): "Let me see how you have done your work," pushing his way through the terrified and weeping girls, whose backs plainly show the cruel thrashing they have received during the process. "Let me see. Ha! Ha! You have not done badly, but after plucking there is always a little which must be singed to make the flesh quite bare; you Flora and Veneria, each hold up a leg and keep them wide apart." Thus assisted he holds the flame of the candle first to the brown orifice of her bottom, blistering and burning in a cruel manner; but the poor girl is quite helpless and unable to do more than slightly moan;

she is even past sobbing and sighing. He next singes all over her mount, opening the lips of her delicate maiden cunny and dropping the burning hot grease from the candle both inside and out during the operation.

He is so excited he can no longer wait, he must enculer the victim at once. His dressing gown is thrown aside, displaying to the horrified girls his lustful weapon; they cover their faces with their hands and crimson again with redoubled shame.

The two women slash right and left to make them look at the scene. Flora is made to help hold up the victim and Veneria is placed kneeling in front of Sir Charles, bathed in tears, with bleeding cuts across her face, and made to moisten his affair in her mouth. The poor girl's shocked modesty and reluctant disgust only add to his excitement; he pushes her over and taking a leg under each arm, Madame directs his pego to Haidee's scorched and blistered hole; it is an awful scene. Flora whilst supporting the victim's body, hugs and kisses her bosom, washing it with her tears; Veneria hides her face on the floor whilst the two youngest, Alice and Sophia try not to see the horrible sight by hiding their tearful crimson faces in each other's bosoms.

Sir Charles, in his furious lust, thrusts on and on, slowly tearing his way into the maiden orifice.

Haidee, although so exhausted, is brought to her full senses by the violent shock and shrieks again and again: "Oh! Oh! Ah! Ah-r-r-re! You monster!" She struggles with what little strength she has to get away from his attack, but it is fruitless; she is too weak. He gains ground, little by little, pushing and tearing; the interior lining membrane of the anus is torn and bleeding, but finally he effects a complete insertion of his inflamed instrument.

Haidee shrieks "Ah-r-r-re!"

Sir Charles: "Ha! Ha! Shriek away Haidee, it adds to my pleasure; it would not be half so exciting if you were dumb. Oh! How deliciously your bottom throbs to my pressure! Ah! Ah! You can't help yourself! There! There! that will ease you a little!" He spends so excitedly that he is quite exhausted, and lays all along his victim in a lethargy of voluptuousness for some moments, till Lucidora draws him away to his chair, whilst Madame and Flora take down poor Haidee and lay her on the floor at the end of the room to recover by herself or wait till they can remove her.

Madame covers her up with a blanket, after pouring a little brandy down her throat, then turning her attention to Sir Charles, assists to make him presentable once more by replacing his dressing gown.

"Now Flora," she says, "whilst Sir Charles rests himself you must tell us a tale."

Flora (throwing herself on her knees): "Oh! Mercy! Madame! How can I relate such things when I never had any experiences of it till now!"

Madame: "You must; you shall!" slashing her across the face with her whip. "You ought to know enough by this time; your mock modesty won't save you!" Striking her again and again till her face is a specimen of ruined beauty and covered with bleeding weals.

Flora (in agony): "Oh! Oh! I would! I would! But how can I? It's impossible! Oh! Madame, have mercy!"

Madame: "You shan't get off so;" putting her hand in her pocket, "you shall read this little tale, it is not much, Sir Charles, but we must make her do something. Now, Flora, do you understand? No squeamishness!"

Flora, trembling, takes the paper, her bleeding face showing how inexpressibly disgusting the task is to her sense of modesty.

Madame: "Now then are you never going to begin! Attention! All hands by your sides," making the other three stand close to Sir Charles' chair, that he may watch their confusion and distress.

Flora, looking over the paper, every unscathed part of her features scarlet with shame, reads:

This is an account of a scene witnessed in a wood by a gentleman who happened to be unseen by the actors evidently father and daughter.

Father: "Come my dear this is a beautifully quiet spot; let me look at your legs."

Daughter: "Oh! Papa, Papa! What do you mean! You can always see my feet and ankles."

Father: "That's nothing, I must see more and teach you to obey me in everything I order; now lift up your skirt."

Daughter (all blushes): "Well then, Papa, there's my legs," drawing up her clothes so as to reveal the ends of finely embroidered drawers. "Is that what you require?"

Father: "Only a portion of what I want to see," handling her calves and putting his hand up her drawers; "you have sweetly proportioned legs and beautifully firm flesh, my dear; up higher with your skirts, please."

Daughter (scarlet with shame): "Oh, oh, Papa! How can you? There only a little higher; that's all I can do; it's so indelicate;" drawing her skirts half way up her thighs.

Father (in a rage): "Do as I tell you, Miss; do you think I can't examine my own child without her pretending to tell me it's improper! I will look you all over if I choose to do so, and whip you soundly in the bargain, Miss Prude."

Daughter (with tears of shame running down her crimson face): "Oh! Papa, Papa! Pity me; I never showed so much to any one before!" lifting her clothes so as now to show all her drawers, well up to her waist, but she stands with her legs so close that nothing is visible.

Father: "That's how you dress is it? It's time I looked after your underclothing a little, your chemise is too long," putting his hand between her legs and pulling out the tail of her under-most garment. "What a pretty little pussey you have my dear little Miss Bashful. I suppose you won't let your husband even look at or touch that; why how beautifully it's covered with this soft hair!" caressing and tickling the pouting lips with his fingers, "and you're only just over sixteen; you must have been rubbing your belly against something hairy."

Daughter (in still greater confusion, turns away from him to hide her mortification, sobbing hysterically): "Oh! Oh! Papa, Papa! Have mercy! How can you talk so?"

Father (taking out his knife): "Stand still Miss Prude, I am going to make this chemise the proper length so as to be a pattern of what you ought to wear." Then cuts a great piece off back and front so as to leave her quite exposed where the drawers are a little open, as he purposely leaves them. "You have a fine, plump bottom; is it tender? Do you feel that?" giving her a loud slap. "Oh! you can feel, can you; does it hurt you much?" as she starts with the sudden smart.

Father: "Now get up, your drawers are only a little soiled," laughing at the great patch of mud on her knees. Take my knife and cut me some of those nice long thin twigs and ask me to correct you with them."

She complies, being too frightened and confused not to obey; the twigs are handed to her father who ties them up into a nice little switch, then orders her to kneel on the ground with her bottom towards him;

makes her with her own hands hold her drawers well open behind for him to inspect her posterior beauties, then makes her pin them back so they will not close over the exposed rump.

Father: "Now, my dear, you would like me to correct you, would you not, Miss Bashful!"

Daughter: "Oh, oh, no, no! Box my ears, anything but that! I've done nothing."

Father: "You must be made to see your own conduct in the right light; ask me to whip you properly," switching her bottom smartly and making long red marks at each stroke. "Tell me you wish it or I'll tickle you more and more with this."

Daughter (screaming with pain): "Oh, oh, oh, ah, Papa! I can't bear it; I can't indeed. Oh! Oh! Yes, correct me properly, dear Papa. Oh! Oh! Have mercy," as he cuts harder and harder, drawing little drops of blood form the tender flesh.

Father: "That's right, my dear, you are just beginning to take it in a proper spirit. Oh, yes, you can bear it. Shriek out, it will do you good," swishing away vigorously and enjoying the wriggling of her rosy coloured bottom as each stroke tells its tale.

The poor girl is almost ready to faint, her bottom smeared with blood from the broken weals, she wants to let down her clothes but he makes her crawl just as she is to the bushes and cut another birch, enjoying every movement; then when she presents the twigs to him he makes her kiss them and tell him "she hopes he will flog her well for his pleasure and her own good."

Father: "That's right my dear, I must cut that prudishness out of you; now open your legs well as you kneel; a little more dear," switching her gently at first; "it hurts me as much as it does you, poor dear," cutting harder and raising more weals on her devoted bum.

Father: "Does that hurt you so much, dear? I think you had better drop your drawers quite down. I must hurt you a little more for your good. That's right, it will do you good," as she screams frantically for "mercy! mercy! Oh! Spare me now, Papa!"

Daughter (sobbing and crying in most humiliated distress): "Oh Papa! Oh! Papa! I've done everything; you do hurt so; you are so cruel! Ah-r-r-re!" as he gives a sharp undercut on her pussey.

Father: "That's right; scream loudly; I couldn't help touching up your poor little pussey;" cutting again and again in the same place and all over her poor naked bottom till it is quite covered with weals and blood-stained all over.

The poor daughter writhes and wriggles with the pain; her sobs and cries get weaker and weaker, till at last she fairly faints.

The sight of her inanimate form seems to bring him back to his natural feeling, for he caresses and kisses her, calling her his darling victim of a daughter, poor thing, poor thing, etc., and as soon as she revives a little conducts her from the scene.

Flora is awfully distressed all through the reading of this tale and has only been kept to her task by the inflexible application of Madame's whip.

Sir Charles: "Come here, Sophie, don't be so shy." Taking her on his knee and feeling the little girl all over; "have they been cruel to you my dear? Let me look at your poor little bottom and see if it's at all bruised." Then laying her across his knee regardless of her drawers behind exclaiming as he does so: "What a beautiful, plump little bum, why, there's nothing the matter with it."

He now proceeds to slap her with his open hand, each blow sounding sharply through the apartment, and echoed by the poor girl's cries for "Mercy! Pity! Mercy! Oh! Oh! Spare me!" The more he slaps the more exciting it is to him to have such a young thing wriggling and writhing under his hands; it seems like another new sensation; then Madame, seeing his excitement rising so rapidly, hands him a very light little birch.

Sophie: "Oh Oh! I can't bear that! Oh! Mercy! Sir Charles!" as he begins to thrash her and making the strokes leave their marks on her already flushed bottom.

Sir Charles: "Does it hurt you so much my little dear? Oh! How I love you; I'm so sorry," still birching in earnest, making the victim shriek more and more at every stroke.

Had it not been a very light birch she would have been cut to pieces, but Madame was anxious to spare the little thing for another time, especially as Sir Charles was too excited to last long. At length the thin twigs are quite worn out and he demands another "enculade," but Madame rescues the victim from his raging lust, for this time, and makes Veneria and Alice come and kneel in front of Sir Charles with bunches of nettles in their hands, and flog and irritate his excited and bursting affair for a few moments till he spends all over their faces.

Sir Charles is fairly exhausted and the séance is brought to a close for the present.

END OF VOL. II.

Part the Third

Arrival of M. de Bonvit From Paris

Two days after their conversazione Madame informs Sir Charles that she has good news; for the Count de Bonvit, who had the adventure with Mrs. Armor and her daughter, has arrived in Constantinople and would make a most agreeable addition to their next séance, if he would like him to be invited.

Sir Charles readily assents to this and the Count is requested by Madame, in her invitation, to come to them at once, as she can insure him as pleasurable an adventure as he had with his lady love in the Pyrenees, and fixes an early day in the ensuing week for his arrival, assuring him that Sir Charles is most desirous of making his acquaintance and hopes he will have a well-stocked repertoire of adventures to amuse them.

The Count, who has come to the East in search of excitement, is only too glad to avail himself of Madame Josephine's pressing invitation, and arrives as soon as he can possibly be expected.

Sir Charles is charmed by his graceful manners and constant fund of racy anecdotes; they speedily open their hearts and feelings to each other and find an extraordinary coincidence in their previous lives and present state of feeling. Sir Charles is anxious for more excitement and the Count longs to experience again the delightful voluptuousness he has only once before been able to realize.

During the afternoon previous to the evening séance, Sir Charles and Monsieur have some confidential conversation in the library after luncheon.

Sir Charles: "Count, what is your opinion about sodomizing young girls?"'

Count: "You know it is a constant practice with Frenchmen and many married men who have no other kind of connection with their wives for fear of getting a family; in fact it is the best of Malthusian checks to over-population."

Sir Charles: "But is it true that many fathers sodomize their own daughters!"

Count: "Yes, Mirabeau's 'Education of Laura' is supposed to be a true tale of himself and daughter; many brothers and sisters practice sodomy in France; it is thought nothing of being harmless in its results, and even occasionally brought to light is passed over in silence."

Sir Charles: "All the girls I have ever had the pleasure to enculer have been virgins in every respect; their resistance, the painful shrieks and awful sense of the humiliating degradation add to my voluptuous fury, and even if I knew I was murdering my own daughter it would not stop my wild lustful excitement, when once aroused by previous castigations and all kinds of shocks to their modesty; to know they have been brought up delicately and even religiously, adds to the zest of the violator; what the novices and sincerely pious nuns must suffer as depicted by De Sade! Do you think there was any real foundation for his writings?"

Count: "I will tell you a real tale about a nun this evening; I knew the heroine a short time ago in Paris; she escaped from a Belgium nunnery and became a famous member of the Parisian demi-monde, and a devil of cruelty herself."

Sir Charles: "How old was she when she entered the convent?"

Count: "About fourteen; when I first knew her she was only eighteen and delighted in all kinds of torture, even inflicted on herself, to excite her lustful feelings."

Sir Charles: "Your tale will be most welcome; you know our poor Maud died under the whip, but I should like to drill Flora and Alice till they take pleasure in flagellation themselves; they would thoroughly understand how to stimulate me and find their own voluptuous enjoyment in catering to my necessary excitement. I have an idea in my head, with respect to Madame and Lucidora, and shall want some one to replace them. You, Count, will not abuse my confidence; they are cruel women and we ought to try them to murder some day, when we can be properly supported."

Count: "Certainly, Sir Charles. Although I have known Madame Josephine a long time, it has only more and more convinced me she ought some day to suffer for all her iniquities; what rapes, seductions and fearful crimes she has had to do with in her time it would be impossible to enumerate."

Sir Charles: "We are agreed then as to some future action and as you have no special engagement to take you elsewhere, I shall keep you with me as a faithful ally. This evening we will devote to the Greek family; my own Flora and Alice shall be compelled to help as much as possible!"

Count: "You have then four victims; what combinations and delicious episodes we shall be able to extract; they will be all virgins to me."

Sir Charles: "Not one has lost her maidenhead, and as to their fundas, that is always so tight and gives such opposition in effecting an entrance and such delicious sensations, pulsations and throbbing contractions that it may truly be said the maidenhead of a bottom is as indestructible as the mythological Phoenix."

Count: "What a voluptuous prospect for a poor roué like me; young, modest, virtuous girls to ravish and humiliate; how different from the complaisant dalliance of the professional courtesans we have both been used to."

Here the conversation dropped for the time, and no more was said, till the whole family was assembled in the lecture room for another séance.

Sir Charles introduces the Count to the young ladies as a particular friend from Paris, the veritable M. de Bonvit, who had the adventure with Mrs. Armor and her daughter; "so you see, my dears," he said, "what an experienced operator and valuable acquisition Monsieur is likely to prove; besides he has promised a most interesting tale of a nun who escaped from a Belgian convent, where she had been fearfully ill-treated."

Count: "Sir Charles, your praises are scarcely warranted by the facts, for I have had only that one experience. Are they all well-behaved, modest and obedient young ladies?"

Sir Charles: "Mademoiselle Haidee, there, is very obstinate; she will be punished again, this evening, unless she is more obedient to our requirements."

Madame, as mistress of the ceremonies, bows to the Count, saying: "Monsieur, as our guest this evening, we hope to afford you a little pleasurable excitement; these six young ladies are all beautiful and accomplished; they have been virtuously, modestly and religiously educated up to the present; would you like to see their beautiful legs?"

Count: "With great pleasure, Madame, but I hope the young ladies do not mind it; as I am a stranger to them all."

Madame makes them all stand on a long low table, covered with green baize, which is only about eighteen inches from the ground; the girls look all quite well, and scarcely a mark is to be seen on their fair shoulders or faces; but as they have to cast off their dresses and reduce themselves to their short under-petticoats, all are visibly shamefaced and blushing at having to do so before a stranger; it is doubtful if Sir Charles had had no friend with him whether the young ladies would have blushed so readily after their previous experiences with him.

Count: "How delightful!" putting an eye glass to his eye and closely surveying the long line of beautiful legs, in silk stockings and elegant high-heeled Parisian boots. He turns to Haidee, who with heightened colour and flashing eyes, shows her indignation; "Mademoiselle will permit me to examine her beautiful legs," said he, passing his hand up her drawers. "Ah! Mademoiselle Haidee, I have heard of the cruel plucking and singeing you were subjected to the other day; will you do me the pleasure of allowing me to examine your injuries? Allow me, mademoiselle, to help you to be seated on the edge of the table," as he gallantly hands her down and places her conveniently for his inspection, with her clothes well raised under her arms and without appearing to notice her confusion and distress, he proceeds to open her drawers in front and putting aside the tail of her chemise, gets a full view of the hairless mount.

Haidee: "Oh! Oh! You are polite, but quite as ruthless and cruel as the others; you only degrade me, to enjoy my confusion.

Count: "Mademoiselle is unjust to me, but I can see

very little evidence of the cruel treatment you suffered only eight days ago; how shameful to deprive you of the lovely covering to your virginity," kissing her mount with great affection and warmth. He gently forces her legs apart and kisses her clitoris. Inserting his tongue as far as possible into the maiden slit he most lasciviously works the velvet tip and now and then gives gentle, loving bites on the excited clitoris; all the while his moustache and beard add greatly to the titillation of the parts and work poor Haidee into a variety of voluptuous and inexpressible sensations; she wriggles about in excitement, and scarcely knowing what she does, presses his head with one hand to keep him at his work, and presently spends with great profusion, to his infinite enjoyment.

Haidee: "Ah! Ah! What have I done! What have you excited me to do?" hiding her face in her hands in the greatest possible confusion.

Count (who had been kneeling between her legs, springs to his feet, exclaiming): "Oh! you charming girl, what pleasure you have given me; I could suck every drop of your virtuous spendings! Ah! Ah! I must kiss you!" Pulling away her hands and pressing his lips to hers, as she vainly strives to avert her crimson face.

Sir Charles: "It's quite contrary to our usual mode of procedure, but, Monsieur le Comte, if it would be such a great gratification to you, no doubt Mademoiselle Haidee would surrender all her virgin charms to such a gallant cavalier; and also afford us a most exciting exhibition as she is so lasciviously disposed."

Haidee (struggling to release herself from the Count's embrace): "Oh! Oh! Spare me! I couldn't help my feelings being so pleasurably excited. Oh! It is shameful! You are indeed an odious man with all your politeness."

Count: "Oh! Haidee, Haidee! How can you be so

cruel and obstinate? Have I not tried to give you pleasure instead of pain?—and how different must such loving, blissful emotion be to the awful pain of a furious whipping. See, see and feel, darling, how you have made me love you!" placing her unwilling hand upon his swelling, distended priapus, which he has let out and already carried close to the virgin fortress.

Sir Charles is delighted, exclaiming: "Let her feel the real cupid's dart; we'll make a fine scene of it. Flora and Veneria shall slap your posteriors with their hands, whilst little Melissa shall kneel behind you and tickle and play with your member as it goes in and out."

Haidee: "Oh! Oh! Ah! Spare me! Kill me, rather! Oh Count! Have you not the least pity for a helpless girl!"

The Count, who has been attired in a dressing gown throws it aside and clasping Haidee round the waist with one arm, reclining her backwards on the table, with her bottom resting on the edge, whilst with the disengaged hand he directs his fiery steed to her slightly gaping cunny, which his previous kissing has well lubricated and succeeds in fixing the purple velvety head within the entrance, exclaiming:

"Now, now, Haidee, dear, meet my charge firmly and I will soon complete your happiness," beginning to shove gently at first, so as to accustom her to the distension of the tender part, which still feels a little of the effects of Sir Charles' previous cruelty.

Haidee, in spite of her indignation and apprehension, feels a luscious, longing warmth of excitement, which she is powerless to repress; her struggles are fainter and less resolute and she sobs hysterically for them to kill her and finish her off; then feeling the pain of his attack, she screams:

"Ah! Ah! Oh! You'll split me! Oh! Horrible! You're killing me! Oh! Oh!"

Count (in ecstasy): "What a delicious fickle-minded girl you are, my darling. You ask me to kill you, and now you scream because it's being done. But you won't die; I shall kill you and drown you with erotic and most voluptuous pleasure. Oh! Oh! I could eat you!" Seizing in his mouth the nipple of one of the exposed globes of her lovely bosom, just as the two girls begin to slap his bottom vigorously and little Melissa also tries her exciting touches, schooled to her duty by Madame's ruthless whip.

Here the scene is most voluptuously interesting; Madame has pinned up the skirts of Flora and Veneria, and furnishing Alice and Sophia with birch rods to keep them up to their work in slapping the Count's buttocks, whilst with her own whip she carries out a general superintendence, especially over little Melissa, who is nearly dead with fear and shame, so awful does the idea of touching such a hot, fiery thing as Monsieur's inflamed instrument seem to her. Besides, she has a fair view of the havoc it is committing on her dear sister, tearing and forcing its way into her belly, advancing and retreating like a battering-ram and all ensanguined from the results of its prowess.

Sir Charles is also terrifically affected; he is constantly changing his position so that the minutest details may not escape his attention and finally settles himself close behind little Melissa, digging his nails into her plump little bum as his excitement increases more and more by the delicious sight of Haidee's ravishment, making the little thing scream in agony "Oh! Oh! Ah-r-r-re! Sir Charles, Oh!" with floods of tears coursing down her pretty little crimson face.

Haidee screams in awful pain: "Ah! Ah! You bite so! Oh my God! I can't bear it. I must die!" as she feels him tearing her vagina and gradually forcing his way through her hymen. "Oh! Oh! Awful! How painful!" She screams again.

The Count shoves on furiously and revels in the delights of Haidee's charms, bursting through all obstacles till he finds himself in complete possession and the poor girl almost fainting from the desperate assault, which has been so painful to her. He rests a little, making his fiery instrument throb inside of her tight-fitting sheath till he feels a slight reciprocation of his pressures which excites him that it is impossible to contain himself longer, and giving her two or three gentle movements so as not to hurt her lacerated vagina, he finishes with a vigorous thrust and remains in her right up to his testicles, throbbing and spending in profusion into her inmost womb and soaking in delight.

Haidee is so eased and lubricated by his copious discharge that all sense of pain and distension gives way to pleasurable excitement and she responds to the throbbing of his weapon by most loving pressures and contractions of her vagina, urging him, in the most lovable manner, to renewed motions, which he is not slow to respond to.

Both now enter into the exciting game, and the victim by her motions, seems literally to rejoice in the loss of her maidenhead, her movements are so rapturous and exciting. She closes her eyes in delirious enjoyment, whilst her lips are lovingly glued to those of the Count, and she excitedly thrusts her tongue into his mouth in response to his previous challenge.

The Count fairly shouts with excess of pleasure: "Ah! Oh! I believe I shall die in her! Oh! delightful Haidee! You will kill me with excitement! Ah! Ah! how my heart beats!" as he spends again a stream of his love essence into her luscious cunny and meets a reciprocating discharge from her. Her arms are now round his waist pressing him to her bosom as they lay in a lethargy of voluptuous exhaustion and she is again urging him to renewed action by the loving pressures of her excited and longing vagina on his still stiff and distended instrument.

Sir Charles: "Ha, ha, ha! Well done, Haidee; you can't enjoy it in the least; let's try another position."

With the assistance of Madame and Lucidora they take the Count off his loving victim, who is scarlet with confusion and prolonged excitement.

"Ah! my dear, you shan't lose him long; we're only going to put him underneath, so that he may not injure himself by such furious exertions. You will have to do all the work and let him lay and enjoy it."

The Count is laid on his back on the table, with a cushion under his head and another under his buttocks, his still excited pego retaining its stiffness all the while, and standing up in its majestic glory, a model of vigorous manhood.

They make Haidee strip off all her clothes, and then quite naked, she first has to kneel upon the table and give the object of her love a luscious sucking, which she does willingly enough, now she has been made to taste its sweets, and takes the head fairly in between her lips, and applying the tip of her tongue to the sensitive surface, soon excites him almost up to the spending point; but Madame, who watches every process, does not allow the game to be spoilt so soon.

She touches Haidee up smartly with the whip, raising quite a weal across her buttocks, and orders her to impale herself on the Count's prick.

Haidee almost jumps with the sudden and unexpected pain, but is willing enough to insert the shaft of love in her longing pussey, where he is soon housed out of sight.

Madame (handing Sir Charles a very beautiful, finely ornamented bunch of birch): "Here, Sir, you can best keep her on the move; you need not be too particular about touching the Count; he is sure to enjoy himself immensely."

Sir Charles: "Thank you, Madame. Now, Haidee—I'm going to add to your pleasure; cling tightly to Monsieur and work your bottom well up and down; you will soon make him in Heaven again," touching her bottom lightly with two or three preliminary switches; then as the skin begins to flush, it excites him to go on in earnest. His blows fall with smarting sharpness on the moving bottom, leaving their tell-tale red marks at every cut.

Haidee: "Ah! Ah! Oh! You'll spoil it all by cutting so hard. Oh! How hot my bottom is! Ah-r-r-re!" as she gets an undercut which switches both her pussey and the shaft of Monsieur's pego.

Sir Charles: "You can't have all the fun to yourselves; didn't you like that cut? Well, perhaps this will be better," watching his opportunity to give another good slashing undercut, just as she raises her bottom and fully exposes the Count's weapon again, this time with such effect that the shaft is slightly blood-stained with the drops that ooze front the lips of her wounded pussey.

The Count cries out in pain, but Haidee fairly shrieks for pity.

"Oh! Oh! Sir Charles, spare me! Have mercy; your cuts are awful! Ah! Oh! Delightful!" as she spends profusely and deluges with her sperm all round the root of his weapon.

The Count also comes again a moment or so after her and they lay in voluptuous exhaustion, regardless of the shower of cuts Sir Charles is raining upon poor Haidee's posteriors, which are now blood-stained all over.

Sir Charles: "Look at that, Madame; they're actually going to sleep in spite of me. Wake up! Wake up will you?" he cries, cutting away, and taking good care to let the Count feel some of his smartest strokes.

The loving couple are soon thoroughly aroused, and the extraordinary warmth of the parts has so sustained their erotic passions that they at once recommence another furious course, to the delight of Sir Charles and the spectators, who are quite enthralled by the sight. Haidee is almost delirious with excitement, and works her bottom up and down on the Count's pego with extraordinary velocity, at the same time her cunny clings to his shaft, with all its delightful contractions, and scarcely gives time to Sir Charles to commence again with the birch (as he has lost time in stopping to enjoy the scene) before she pumps Monsieur up to the spending point once more and they die away again in an excess of pleasure.

The Count is quite exhausted, and at a motion from Sir Charles, Madame and her assistant remove the excited and lascivious Haidee, her vagina clinging to the Count's priapus to the last, and seems quite reluctant to lose its loving prisoner; who, however, is quite done with for the present.

Sir Charles: "Ha! Ha! Ha! Why Haidee, who would have thought it of you going on so and almost ravishing Monsieur," whisking his birch about; "fie, fie, Miss Lecherous! I should like to give you a good thrashing now, but will let you off if you only give a fair description of your late emotions."

Haidee, slightly recovered from her erotic excitement, is all blushes and confusion, now she finds it is all over, and how she has displayed her voluptuous inclinations before the assembled company: "Ah! indeed, Sir Charles, you ought to pity me; how could I help myself? The Count first put me in a dreadful pain as he burst through all my virgin defences, then waiting for the distension to subside, he lubricated my inside with such a copious discharge of his beautiful soothing fluid, which to my heated and lacerated parts proved a veritable elixir of life. I revived all at once and felt his movements within me; they threw me into such a state of voluptuous erotic (I suppose you would call it) longing to feel him more and more; every moment the feeling was so delicious and pleasurable, every thrust threw me into greater confusion, but it was not a confusion of shame, rather a wild loving desire to hasten I knew not what, which culminated when I met his next discharge with an overflow of my own essence of love, and we both fell into a lethargy of oblivious bliss; your blows seemed dull and only added to our pleasurable warmth, and with me a still increasing longing for more, more, more, ever more of the same bliss; Oh! Oh! that it had never ended, but men fail if women do not; oh! Sir Charles, why are we so much more excitable than you men?"

Sir Charles: "Bravo! Bravo! Haidee; I can't punish you again after such a feeling account of your love passage; we all want a little rest; perhaps Madame can amuse us for a time with something from her repository of Lascivious Gems."

Madame: "I won't trouble you with foolish excuses, but begin to tell you a tale of Henri Quatre, the gallant Le Bearnais, first a Protestant then a Catholic; his only religion was the love of women, which gradually brought him to such a reduced state of manly vigour that he had to have recourse to all sorts of lascivious ideas for excitement, especially his plan of being frigged before and behind by little boys, which I will not further allude to, as I think it is an objectionable topic to the present company; at any rate my story relates to a period antecedent to that in which he had recourse to his little Cupids, as he called them.

Now for my tale. For a long time after the crown devolved upon him he had to fight for its possession; his bitterest foes were the Duke of Mayenne and his sister, Mademoiselle de Montpensier who contested his supremacy; they defended Paris against him till the inhabitants were reduced to skeletons, and only finally escaped by the arrival of the relieving Spanish army under the celebrated Duke of Parma, who compelled Henri to retire from the siege. Mortified beyond measure by his failure before the capital of his kingdom, he meditated revenge of a different sort. Mademoiselle de Montpensier was a very virtuous bigoted Romanist, a beautiful brunette of about seven and twenty, and King Henri longed to possess and humiliate her, if he could by any possibility get her into his power, even for a short time. Her brother, the Duke, left Paris immediately the siege was raised, in order to rouse his partisans in the country and risk another campaign against the King, who had hitherto been invariably victorious over the Catholic leaguers.

"This was the opportunity for Henri; he immediately devised and caused a forged letter, purporting to come from the Duke of Mayenne, to be sent to Mademoiselle, requesting her to meet her brother secretly in a wood near Charenton, and to come disguised as a peasant girl, for fear of the royal troops, and he would meet her as a simple cavalier, to give her special instructions for the preservation of Paris and how to divert the attention of the King's army from himself, as long as possible, and so enable him to take the field with a prospect of success.

The forgery was so cleverly executed and delivered with such a show of diplomatic secrecy that

Mademoiselle de Montpensier was completely deceived. She hastened to the rendezvous next day, having to meet her brother at a certain hermitage in the depths of the forest, well known to both brother and sister for the sanctity of its occupant.

Henri had caused the old hermit to be removed to a place of safety and himself, disguised as a holy man, awaited the arrival of his unsuspecting victim. It was getting towards mid-day of a fine July morning when the disguised monarch spied a pretty young peasant woman approaching the hermitage. His heart beat with increased force and a thrill of exultation ran through his veins as he recognized the beautiful de Montpensier and felt assured of his victim.

Peasant girl (approaching the cell of the recluse, addresses the hermit): "Holy Father, methinks you are not the celebrated Anthony, who inhabits this sanctified retreat. Can you tell me were he is or if you have seen a cavalier near here this morning?"

Hermit: "The blessing of the Virgin be with you, my girl; if you came to confess to Father Anthony, he is gone to pray with a sick man at Dreux and I have taken his place for a day or two; but if you are bent upon some sinful assignation with a cavalier, a gallant looking gentleman came to me an hour ago. See, here" (holding out his hand with a couple of gold pieces in the palm) "he gave me this for charity, and desired me to lead a peasant girl who might inquire for him, to a secluded glade not far from here, where he would await our coming and rest his wearied steed."

Peasant Girl: "Thanks, thanks, Holy Father; we are not what we seem; ours is no sinful assignation, but one fraught with good for the cause of our beloved Catholic religion; lead on, my brother will reward you yet more."

Hermit: "We have only to follow the hoof marks of

his horse and shall soon find him; come on, maiden, and may good prosper our consultation. Methinks, now I look at you, you are marvellously like the Lady Princess Mademoiselle de Montpensier, and the cavalier must be the gallant, noble Duke, your brother."

Peasant Girl: "Hush! Hush! Holy Father. Your garb makes us trust your discretion, but even trees have ears sometimes; lead on; our time is precious."

The King walks by her side in silence, for several hundred yards into the densest part of the forest, until by following the trail of the horse they arrived at a small open glade, surrounded by trees and shrubs on every side, affording them a choice of sunshine or shade, as they may prefer. A finely caparisoned horse is tied under one of the oak trees, but no signs of a cavalier; only the accoutrements and cloak of a gentleman lay on the grass, close to the steed. Mademoiselle is evidently perplexed at the absence of her brother, and suddenly looking at her companion, she turns pale at seeing him throw aside his disguise and appear before her as a gentleman.

"What! What is the meaning of this?" she cries in confusion. "Am I in a trap?"

Gentleman: "Most undoubtedly fair lady, you thought to see Mayenne, but behold in me your hated enemy, Henri Quatre; you are entirely in my power; is it not a pleasant situation to find yourself alone, tête-à-tête, with one who has such a gallant reputation, my modest, virtuous Mademoiselle de Montpensier?"

Mademoiselle, her face scarlet with rage and indignation: "How infamous! Know, heretic that you are, I despise you and spit on you!" suiting the action to the word.

Henri (avoiding the expectoration): "Gently, gently, fair lady, or you will compel me to handle you roughly;

if you comply with all my orders I shall let you go presently; otherwise you have nothing to expect but a horrible death; I mean to have my revenge now, and it will rest with you if it is ever known to any beyond our two selves."

Mademoiselle: "Usurper, what do you mean; are you going to commit any violence upon me!" as the reality of her situation becomes more and more apparent to her.

Henri: "You will see; in the first place it is not proper for such a lady to wear the dress of a peasant girl; observe this whip; obey instantly; discard those improper habiliments or I shall hasten your obedience by the application of the lash to every part of your body."

Mademoiselle (flushing this time with shame and apprehension): "I have nothing else to wear; you will never make me strip when I have no other change of clothing!"

Henri: "I have provided for all that; my dignity will not allow me to have any conference with you till you assume more becoming attire for such an exalted, proud lady," whisking the whip about. "Now, make haste; no further delay or I slash you!"

Mademoiselle, now fully aware of her hopeless situation, throws herself upon her knees. "Oh! Oh! Sire! I am helpless; have mercy; permit me to make the change behind those bushes; I will pledge my word to obey and dress quickly."

Henri (laughing ironically): "No faith with heretics is the motto of your church; do you think I would trust to your most solemn oath? Undress before me this instant; I will not lose sight of you for one moment; I shall derive the greatest possible pleasure from your humiliation and distress," seeing the tears stand in her eyes and the contention between fear and indignation in her countenance. "How do you like that? I shall waste no more words upon a peasant girl," giving her a sharp cut with the whip over her shoulders as she kneels before him.

Mademoiselle feels the lash for the first time in her life; her delicate shoulders smart and tingle from the force of the blow, although protected by her peasant's dress; but still in her confusion she cannot decide to obey at once; her feelings are so repugnant to the exposure and degradation and she merely screams: "Ah! Ah-r-r-re! Oh! Have pity, Sire!" but the whip falls again and this time her tender neck is wealed and bruised; she is in dreadful pain and holds up her hands to avert the blows, but to no purpose. The King is regardless of what damage he may do to such a delicate lady and cuts away till she screams again and again for mercy, promising to comply with his orders.

Henri is greatly excited by her distress. "Wretched traitress," he exclaims, "don't hope to be let off easily. You were privy to the Massacre of Saint Bartholomew, you are one of the perjured Romanists, who consider anything justifiable to gain your ends. No matter what you have to do with me you can get absolution, or if you prefer it, I will don the Hermit's garb again and absolve you myself better than even the Pope could do it Ha! Ha! I mean to make you drink the very dregs of humiliation before I let you go off with your clothes; you can't help yourself," slashing her again and again and not even sparing her face.

Mademoiselle: "Oh! Oh! Mercy! I will obey if you spare my life!" sobbing hysterically and trying to preserve her face from the brutal attack by interposing her bruised and bleeding hands.

Henri: "Then stand up and undress; pull off that odious, ugly-looking peasant girl's jacket; off with those sabots and coarse woollen stockings."

The lady is too dreadfully cowed by his furious whipping to longer delay her compliance; she hastily gets to her feet and with downcast eyes, crimson face and tears of shame, throws off the outer jacket and displays the delicate lace of her chemisette, just partially concealing the glories of a beautiful rounded bosom, also a fine blue satin corset, laced up behind with silver cord; her coarse skirts are dropped to the ground and Henri is delighted as she stoops to slip off the woollen stockings and sabots, discovering a beautiful pair of flesh-coloured silken hose underneath; also very soft linen trousers or drawers, fitting tightly to the thighs, trimmed with Valenciennes lace, but coming only half way down her thighs, so as to leave a beautiful piece of white flesh exposed between them and the garter line of her stockings. Her jarretieres are composed of gold thread with diamond buckles.

She is now reduced to her corset, chemisette, tight under-drawers and flesh-coloured stockings, without shoes; and the King gloats over the delightful sight, pretending to pity her, etc.

Henri: "Ah! Mademoiselle, how sorry I am; you compelled me to be so rough with such a lady; how your poor shoulders are cut and bruised; you are an angel now, compared to the peasant girl I was obliged to subdue and make obedient."

Mademoiselle, in spite of her indignation, is flattered by his admiration, for she is indeed a splendid woman; she almost smiles and tries to hide her blushing face in her hands. "Ah! Sire! How could you be so cruel to a Lady of the Royal Family of France," she faintly lisps.

Henri fetches his cloak and a pretty pair of slippers, and, making her sit down upon his garment: "Allow me, Mademoiselle, to put these on," he says, proceeding to handle her legs under pretence of helping her to assume her shoes which are so delicately small and petite they almost seem fit for a fairy. "Ah! I knew you had the smallest foot in France; permit me to kiss it, raising one foot to his lips; there, now, see, the pretty shoes fit beautifully. How I wish I had some garments to array you in; you must be uncomfortable in such a state of demi-toilette; what beautiful legs you have," feeling and pinching her calves; "and oh! the firm, marble flesh of your thighs," passing his hands up higher. "You wear culottes. Mademoiselle; they are most objectionable things; they hide such charms from the sight," feeling higher and higher, to the great alarm and distress of the lady, who attempts to repulse him and is scarlet with shame and humiliation.

Mademoiselle: "Ah! Sire! I am indeed in your power. Oh!—have—have—mercy. Spare my honour," sobbing hysterically.

Henri (ironically): "Your honour! Have you got any to lose! I always thought the Romanist Fathers or Confessors took care of that for their fair penitents. Ha! Ha! Ha! I will see and assure myself of your virginity!" attempting to place his hand on the seat of honour; but she nips her thighs together and struggles desperately to avoid his advances.

Mademoiselle: "Ah! you base man, would you ruin me?" her tearful eyes flashing with indignation and shame.

Henri: "By Jove! I'll take down your proud spirit! You promised to obey all my orders and now dare to resist!" springing to his feet and seizing his whip; "on your knees, naughty rebel; I was forgetting myself in making love to you; you have brought me to my senses; why should I ask for what is in my power? Take off that corset!" slashing her with his whip across her thighs and again over her unprotected shoulders, cutting and bruising the tender, delicate flesh.

Mademoiselle: "Ah! Ah! Ah-r-r-re!" with a prolonged scream of agony. "Oh! I am helpless in your hands; strip me; give your orders. I—I—I will do anything," sobbing with fear and pain.

Henri, beside himself with delight at her suffering and sense of degradation, can hardly restrain his whip, the sight of the red weals on her neck and shoulders makes his blood course with unusual warmth through his veins, raising his rather slothful member to an unwonted stiffness and he feels as if he must spend soon.

"Here, you bloodthirsty Romanist," he exclaims, kneel in front of me and take my manly instrument in your mouth or I will murder you on the spot," displaying his now rampant pego in all its pristine glory, to her horrified gaze.

His victim is so terrified she represses her disgust as well as possible and obeys his repulsive command, but she has scarcely got the purple head in her mouth before she is almost choked by a tremendous spend, as he furiously thrusts his instrument forward and holds her head with his hands so that she cannot withdraw her face; she gasps for breath and is ready to faint from the sudden shock and nausea, doing all she can to get rid of the nasty stuff out of her mouth to his great delight, and he finishes off by making her wipe his slimy affair with her beautiful dark brown hair which is hanging loose round her neck. At length recovering herself a little she sobs out:

"Oh! Oh! Horrible! Let me go now; you have humiliated me indeed," hiding her face in her hand again.

Henri: "Not yet, proud lady Now take off your chemisette, I want to admire all your charms, now that you have cooled my ardour a little I shall get excited

again bye and bye and will make you relieve my
sensuality in some different way when the time
comes," gently switching her with the whip to make
her obey quickly, "I feel a little more kindly towards
you after that gamahuche."

Mademoiselle: "Oh! have pity! Let me go! Any
ransom you may demand shall be paid; only name
your terms and spare my life and honour," still hiding
her downcast, crimson countenance to prevent him
enjoying her discomfiture.

The King is impatient and gives her a sharp cut to
show he is not the mind to hold any parley with her,
and she hastily slips off the chemisette, standing
before him with nothing but her tight-fitting drawers
as a slight protection to her modesty. She has a
beautiful figure, rather above the medium height; most
voluptuously developed, with full, rounded bosom,
ornamented with an inviting pair of dark brown
nipples; very slender in the waist, and large well-
rounded buttocks, which are slightly covered by the
close-fitting drawers, the latter being slightly open
behind, so as just to show the crack of her bottom.

Henri: "I must have you sans culottes, Mademoiselle; they hide the most delicious part of your
lovely person; you're continually appealing to me to
save your honour and I have not yet even assured
myself of the existence of your virginity," forcing her to
lie back at full length on his cloak and helping her to
pull off the obstructive drawers.

"By heavens! What a delicious looking mount; what
lovely black curly hair; your honour is beautifully
ornamented, I must confess," opening her reluctant
thighs, and parting the chevelure of her cunny, so as
to give him a full view of the pouting vermilion lips and
most luscious looking clitoris, just projecting a little
between them. He pinches it lasciviously with his

fingers and then, thrusting his forefinger as far as he can up the crack soon assures himself that she is indeed a virgin.

"Ha! Ha! I've found your honour; but have you never been tickled here by any one before now!" continuing his lascivious touches and putting her into great confusion.

Mademoiselle: "Oh! Oh! How disgusting! How indelicate! Oh! Will you never have mercy and let me go?" bursting into tears of shame, which course down her blushing cheeks.

Henri: "I like to hear you cry for mercy; it's delightful, and quite musical to my ears; shriek out, it will do you good and keep your spirits from failing. Ah! You little thought at the time of the massacre of Saint Bartholomew that you yourself might some time have to cry for pity to a relentless persecutor. I love your inviting charms, but have not the slightest feeling for the proud, cruel woman they belong to."

Here he puts his face close to her cunny and thrusts his tongue well into the luscious crack, sucking her clitoris and exciting her erotic passions so that she cannot possibly contain herself but spends a torrent of thick creamy virgin love juice right over his mouth and moustache.

He licks it up with great gusto, and is so excited himself that he gives her several most painful bites on her clitoris and evidently quite enjoys the taste of her blood as it oozes from the deep marks of his teeth.

She screams in agony.

"Ah! Ah! Ah-r-r-re! You're biting me to death! Oh!" Sobbing, crying and screaming with awful shrieks, she clutches at his hair in her frenzied efforts to save herself from his tormenting teeth, and makes him still more furious at her resistance.

He throws himself at full length upon her naked

body, and clasping her waist with his right arm, fixes himself well between her distended legs, and with the left hand directs his inflamed priapus to her virgin gap. It is so well lubricated that he has no difficulty in inserting the head of his affair and is well placed in a most favourable position, almost before she is aware of his projected attack. She desperately tries to wriggle herself from his embrace, but he is too powerful for her and manages to keep his place in spite of all her efforts to dislodge him. Being strong, and a good general as well, he simply waits until she is almost exhausted, and then seizing his advantage, ruthlessly charges her hymen with Cupid's battering ram, which her struggles and resistance have only tended to make still more lustful and impetuous.

Mademoiselle (with a shriek of intense pain): "Ah! Ah! Ah-r-r-re! I'm undone! You will ruin me, you monster. Ah! Ah! Awful!" as she feels him bursting into her vagina and fairly pants under her excruciating pain.

The King is delighted and revels in her inmost charms, regardless of the suffering of his victim. Assured of his victorious assault, he rests a little to recover himself and prolong his enjoyment. Besides he hopes the throbbing of his weapon in her tight-fitting sheath will presently arouse all her lustful pro-pensities, when the first feeling of pain and distension has subsided a little. Then, recommencing with gentle movements, he opens the lips of her cunny with his fingers as wide as possible, so that the hair round the roots of his pego can go well inside, and add to her excitement. He also wets one finger and works it well in her bottom hole, so that presently she awakes as if from a most pleasurable dream, exclaiming:

"Oh! Oh! Beautiful! Where am I?" and he feels the loving contractions of her excited vagina on his instrument and before she is quite awake responds to the challenge and raises all her voluptuous feelings to a pitch of longing excitement she is not able to control. His enjoyment is immense; the resistance he has encountered, added to the sense of triumph over his ravished and degraded victim, have so roused all his lustful sensations that he comes again now with another profuse spend, deluging her vagina with the delicious soothing injection, which she reciprocates by meeting him with an equally impetuous flood of joy, clinging to him in a delirium of ecstasy, with sighs and gasps of pleasure.

Henri (exultingly withdrawing his pego, as he exclaims): "I've won another victory; what a delicious woman; how lusciously she clings to me at the last, when her passions were aroused."

Mademoiselle lies on her back in a listless state, ashamed of opening her eyes to encounter the triumphant gaze of her ravisher.

Henri gives her very little time to indulge in either pleasurable or remorseful feelings; he puts his finger into her cunny and withdraws it all smeared with blood and semen, which he wipes across her mouth, as he says:

"Taste that, it is the essence of our mingled joys. What! you object to it? Ha! Ha! Ha!" laughing at her expression of disgust and mortification; you are low-spirited at having lost what you call your honour and want reviving; lets put on your drawers again," assisting her as she eagerly pulls them on, in her readiness to hide the scene of her ravishment.

Mademoiselle: "Ah! Ah! You have torn and abused me; Oh! have mercy and let me go now; what more can you want from a degraded, defenceless woman?" crying piteously at the thoughts of her humiliation and how she apparently enjoyed it with him.

Henri: "Fie! Fie! I thought you had more resolution and fortitude under misfortune; everything is fair in love or war; what's the use of crying for the maidenhead you can never recover? You want some amusement to distract your thoughts; now kneel down, with your bottom towards me: yes, that's it: you may hide your face in your hands if you please; how tightly your drawers fit over your beautiful and splendidly developed buttocks, just showing the crack of your bottom, where they are open behind: now pay attention, and be quick to do everything but the present," giving her a couple of smart strokes with his whip, across her tightened rump. "I hope I don't hurt you very much; now, tell me truly, did you not enjoy our embrace? Would you not like me to repeat it now?" cutting three or four more times on her bent bottom, each one harder than the other, making her wince and flinch, but she obstinately refuses to answer, and keeps silent.

The King soon gets out of patience and cuts furiously; his blows raise great weals and begin to draw the blood, so that at last she screams in agony: "Oh! Oh! Oh! You're killing me now. Oh! My God! Oh! Holy Virgin! Spare me!"

"Ha! Ha! Ha!" he laughs, "I thought you had lost your tongue; will you tell me now; can you deny that I gave you pleasure; speak the truth or I will cut on till you die under my blows!"

Mademoiselle (in great agony and distress, scarlet with shame and mortification): "Ah! Ah! Oh! You know it all; how could I help my natural feelings? Oh! Ah! Let me go, in mercy, have pity now!" she cries hysterically, sobbing as if her heart would break.

Henri: "You have not half answered my questions; do you not wish me to repeat it?" slashing away and cutting both drawers and flesh into ribbons, taking care that the fine end of his whip shall cut between the tender parts of her thighs and even the lips of her pussey.

Mademoiselle: "Ah! Oh! Yes! Yes! Anything rather than this fearful cruelty!" throwing herself on her belly to avoid the whip curling round her too much and writhing in agony.

Henri: "Now then, pull open the cheeks of your bottom and let me see what sort of a fundus you have; make haste!" keeping his whip at work on her ribs for a change.

Mademoiselle is in such terror and distress she readily obeys in hope of obtaining some alleviation of her torments; she pulls open the cheeks of her bum and shows him the beautiful little hole all surrounded with dark wrinkled skin and quite a pretty fringe of black hair; the sight is maddening; he longs to get into it; the prospect is so deliciously inviting. Restraining himself however, for a while, and wetting his finger, he intensely disgusts her by beginning to give her a bottom frig and soon develops her sensuality once more in spite of her unwillingness. "Ha! Ha! Ha!" he laughs. "You can't help showing your feelings; have you never had a finger or anything else there before today?"

Mademoiselle: "Oh! How you tease me; you know my blood is so heated I can't restrain my feelings. Oh! Oh! indeed you are the first to violate me there except— except—!"

Henri: "Speak up!" giving her raw bottom a smarting spank with his open hand, which elicits a scream of agony. "Why don't you speak up; what do you mean by—except—except—?"

Mademoiselle: Ah! Oh! one of my maids once persuaded me to try a godemiche on myself there; but I didn't like; oh! ah! I thought it so disgusting." as he slaps her again in a most painful manner.

Henri: "No, of course you didn't understand; perhaps you never warmed the instrument and it felt cold; but you shall feel my living godemiche it will give you most exquisite pleasure. 'Tis said that the bottom is the forbidden fruit Adam and Eve were prohibited from tasting; it is so delicious to those who have really tasted it;" here he again produces his distended cock and proceeds to attack the tightly contracted orifice, but notwithstanding his previous frigging, which has well lubricated the entrance, he experiences the greatest difficulty, and is some time before he succeeds in getting the head of his affair fairly inserted; it is so painful to her and she shrieks and wriggles to avoid him, making him more lustful and desperately furious; thrusting and ramming his pego, with all his force, so as to hurt her intensely; but his efforts gradually force the sphincter muscle to give way and at last he is fairly lodged, quite an inch within her anus.

She shrieks fearfully: "Ah! Oh! Ah-r-r-re! You're rending me in pieces! Oh! my God! I must die! How awful! What a big monster your affair is, to burst and tear like that!" as she feels him now getting further and further at each push.

Her cries and screams only add to his maddened lust, her pain gives him exquisite pleasure, he drives more furiously than ever and in a few seconds his big ravisher is housed, right up to the roots.

Assured of possession, he rests a little to give time for the pain to subside, enjoying the heat of her luscious bottom and the delicious throbbings and contractions on his delighted cock, and then putting both his hands on her cunny, and nipping and frigging in front, he, with gentle movements, works her up to the highest pitch of excitement, so that at last they both spend together with screams of delight. After remaining in her bottom for some time and enjoying the throbbings and contractions of the love combat, he is compelled to withdraw, and sits down by her side quite exhausted, whilst she, still raging with unsatisfied desire, throws herself on his neck and kisses him fondly, exclaiming: "Ah! Sire! You have indeed subdued me and made me your loving subject for the future; oh! that such heavenly bliss should so soon come to an end," looking dejectedly at his limp affair and handling it in a hopeless effort to revive its manly vigour.

The King is quite satisfied with his revenge and reluctantly parts from his victim. The result of this adventure being a speedy pacification of his kingdom by his own embracing the Romanist faith, which he did in reality, that he might be able to continue his liaison with Mademoiselle de Montpensier, and continued in blissful connection with her till his life was cut short by the assassin's dagger.

Sir Charles: "It's a fine tale; Haidee's experience has been much the same as that of Mademoiselle. What do you say Haidee? will you be a helper in our amusements in future, now you have experienced the sweets to be enjoyed, by raising such erotic excitement?"

Haidee: "Oh! Dear Sir Charles, you may command me in anything that is to lead up to such joys as I have felt this evening; how exciting Madame's story has been; see. Monsieur is almost ready again;" handling and pulling back the foreskin of the Count's fast-rising pego. "I'm afraid the monster will insult me again," giving it a good slap with her hand. "You impudent fellow, why don't you keep quiet?"

Madame (interposing): "Haidee, Haidee; be moderate, the Count wants properly exciting before he can be fit to satisfy you again; besides, he has to relate the promised story about the Belgian nun; we must let him rest a little longer, whilst we attend to Sir Charles' amusement for a short time."

Sir Charles: "That's right, Madame, you will see to the programme; the episode between the Count and Haidee was not anticipated in our arrangements, but it turned out a delightful incident. We want something piquant; Sophie and Melissa shall be horsed by Veneria and Alice; put nice thin drawers on their charming little bums and let Haidee and Flora try their skill in cutting them open with a good birch, whilst we have a little champagne and a cigar, to refresh ourselves."

The two little victims burst into tears, and cry for mercy, imploring Sir Charles to let them off, and have two of the bigger ones, who are better able to bear it, but without avail, as Veneria and Alice are soon ready for their riders, and at Sir Charles' suggestion (instead of standing) are seated crosswise on chairs, with their backs to the company, and with nothing on but their drawers, which of course are opened as wide as possible behind, to add the beauties of their posteriors to the scene.

The struggling, tearful little girls are stripped and fitted with very tight thin drawers, and as further ornament, Madame says they shall be in full evening dress, producing two elegant little costumes, made of brilliant coloured tissue papers, in which they look quite lovely, and each is given a pretty bouquet of real roses, to hold in their hands, as they make their curtseys to Sir Charles, and falteringly ask him, "if he is pleased to see them have a ride, and hope Haidee and Flora will soon cut off their dress for them." They are quickly mounted on their steeds, and Sir Charles motions for proceedings to commence.

Madame hands the two operators a couple of beautiful light birches, made of long thin twigs, elegantly tied up with crimson and gold ribbons; the victims first have to kiss the rods, their starting tears and scarlet faces, already showing the state of apprehension they are in.

Haidee (evidently delighted at the part she has to take): "What a pair of pretty little dears! Sophie dear, I hope I shan't hurt you much; pray cry out sharply, if I do;" beginning to switch at the tissue paper skirts, which quickly fly in all directions at the touch of the birch, and very soon leave nothing but the thin drawers to protect the tender little bottoms. Flora is equally busy with little Melissa, and the two young ladies, every now and then, take care to cut on the exposed rumps of Veneria and Alice, to make them spring out, and add to the excitement of the scene.

Melissa: "Ah! Oh! I can't bear it! Oh! oh! Flora, you cut so hard!"

Sophie: (joining in the shrieks) "Ah! Oh! Mercy! I shall die!"

They sob and cry and would willingly fall off, if it were possible, but the horses hold them tight on their backs, for fear of the consequences; Haidee and Flora, warm with the excitement of their work, and cut away unmercifully, tearing and fraying the delicate material of the drawers, and scoring the tight little bottoms with dark red marks and weals. Sir Charles and the Count both get terribly excited, especially when the little crimson drops of blood begin to ooze from the bursting weals, as the rods continually bruise the same parts over and over again.

The victims are in fearful agony, but get no respite; fresh rods are handed to their tormentors, who seem as much delighted as the gentlemen at the havoc they are committing and cut away till, as the little girls are almost ready to faint, Sir Charles shouts for them to desist! He rises from his chair, and approaching little Sophia, pretends to sympathize with her in her distress, passing his hand over her poor, raw-looking bottom and putting his face so close to it that the red-hot end of his cigar burns her flesh and makes her plunge in agony.

Pretending not to know what he had done he exclaims: "What's the matter my little dear? How you start; have they hurt you so?" The victim screams fearfully for he purposely keeps letting the hot cigar burn the lacerated skin.

The Count also amuses himself with pinching and nipping the little Melissa tormenting her in an excruciating manner, as he seems to be commiserating her pitiable condition.

Haidee is as much excited as Monsieur and determines not to be balked of her satisfaction; she seizes Melissa, and reclining herself backward on the table, so that her tongue can revel in the delights of the tender bottom, and challenges the Count to ravish her again, whilst he can suck her sister's delicious little cunny with his mouth.

Monsieur is not slow to avail himself of this beautiful conjunction and delights Haidee once more by plunging his now rampant pego into her longing gap, so lusciously exposed to his attack.

Sir Charles, in the meantime, makes Veneria hold tight to Sophie, as she rises from her chair and then reclining forward over the edge of the table, presents to his choice two bottoms to "enculer," so he chooses the elder sister preferring to bottom-frig the little one, whilst his cock is enjoying the other. (They are both virgin orifices).

Veneria is a finely developed girl, and well able to sustain his attack, but the pain attending his first attempts makes her scream sharply: "Oh! Oh! Ah-r-r-r-e! You're hurting me awfully! Oh! Oh! It's awful!" as she finds he has got the head of his affair a little way in; then again as he excitedly plunges forward to complete his conquest, she cries out: "Oh! Oh! I'm torn and split!" throwing herself flat on the table and nipping her bottom closely upon his pego, to check the further advance. Her cries and contractions make him mad with delight; he rests a moment and amuses himself by wetting his fore finger and working it well in Sophie's little brown hole, throwing the child into terrible confusion and making her crimson deeper than ever at the sense of shame.

The Count and Haidee have already enjoyed one voluptuous spend and are speeding on towards another, when Sir Charles, fearing he may be quite left behind in the erotic race charges down to get complete possession of Veneria's bottom and regardless of her shrieks tears and bursts his way into her bowels and lubricates her with a warm discharge of sperm just as Haidee and Monsieur faint away again into a lethargy of voluptuousness; but Sir Charles keeps to his work and excites Veneria till she fairly screams with pleasure and meets his next emission with a warm juicy flow of her own.

Madame seeing both gentlemen are fairly exhausted, makes them all compose themselves as comfortably as possible and then handing the Count another bumper of champagne, calls upon him to keep his promise and relate the story of the Belgian nun.

Monsieur: "I am indeed so greatly indebted to you all for the exquisite pleasures I have tasted this evening that it would be both bad manners and base ingratitude not to do my best to entertain the company a little."

Well, then, to begin. The young lady's name was

Lisette Handelitte; her mamma was a very pious lady of about fifty. Madame Handelitte had been a widow for some years and some of her neighbours asserted she would also have been childless but for the hardworking Fathers of her beloved church, who are generally very assiduous in cases of barrenness in any of the female members of their congregations.

Lisette was a beautiful, fair young girl of nearly fourteen and the Cure of their commune was in reality her papa.

Sir Charles, I don't know if you have ever been in that priest-ridden country, but when in Brussels a stranger cannot fail to remark that there are at least hundreds of women to one man when the people are seen coming out of church, after service; in fact the male portion of the Belgian nation (more especially in the large cities) leaves all the religion to their wives and daughters and the priest amply consoles the neglected spouses, for the erotic fancies of their husbands, who invariably seem to prefer any other women to their own wives. Lisette from an early age was thoroughly imbued with an infallible faith in Holy Mother Church and all belonging to it, and took in good part all the curious and disgusting inquiries of her confessor which the priests invariably make use of in the cases of girls arriving at the age of puberty. Masturbation and libidinous ideas are rigidly inquired after; affectedly for the purpose of rooting out such things from the minds of pure girls but in reality only to feed their own lecherous and prurient conceptions.

A young priest once laughingly assured me as we sat having a confidential chat over a bottle of wine, after a good dinner, that he often frigged himself in the confessional and now and then had a delicious enculade with a pretty girl, always avoiding the front for fear of accidents; and also that it was quite usual for some particular ladies to insist upon having young and handsome priests as confessors; "so, you see, my dear fellow," said he, "I have not dropped into such a very bad thing after all by being forced into the church against my will. No family, no anxieties, good living and plenty of voluptuous enjoyment; in fact, we try, as much as possible, to realize heaven here upon earth, so as to make sure of it."

Well, Lisette thought nothing of it till one day her mamma told her she must prepare for her first communion and would have to attend their Cure at his private residence for instruction. In a day or two she found herself tête-à-tête with Monsieur le Cure, in his study as he called it; but which seemed to her a curious sort of apartment; the old priest sat by a table on which stood a bottle and glasses; there were no signs of a book in the room, but the windows were heavily curtained and there also lay on the table a long brown paper packet besides a small scourge of thin whipcord, tipped with points like little pins, whilst at one end of the room a pair of iron hooks projected from the ceiling, ornamented with small ropes, blocks and pulleys.

Lisette regarded all this with a stare of wonder, but the Cure soon broke the silence by saying: "My daughter, your mother is most anxious you should undergo a thorough preparation for your first communion and has sent you here in order that I may so prepare your mind, by prayer and penance, that you may indeed be worthy of presentation before our Reverend Lord Bishop at the fitting time. Now let me examine you a little."

Cure: "How old are you?"

Lisette: "I shall be fourteen next August."

Cure: "Have you always striven to keep worldly thoughts out of your mind, especially on holy days?"

Lisette: "I learn my catechism and study 'The Garden of the Soul'."

Cure: "Do you ever think about getting married?"

Lisette; "Sometimes; I should like to be happy."

Cure (frowning seriously): "Most improper; when did you think about it last!"

Lisette (innocently): "As I was coming here; it was such a beautiful day and a pair of doves in a tree made me think of it."

Cure (angrily): "What wicked ideas considering the errand you were on; pray have you a sweetheart?"

Lisette: "Mamma does not know it, but it is Alphonse Coueou; the birds accidentally pronounced his name Coueou."

Cure: "You must give up all that; now promise me you won't think of him again."

Lisette (crimsoning with indignation): "Oh! Impossible! Impossible! Reverend Father does God forbid us to love?"

Cure: "How can I begin to prepare you properly when you refuse to put such thoughts away! See—I am prepared—I had guessed as much," taking up the brown paper parcel and producing from it a long switch of green twigs wrapped up in a horse-hair body garment such as penitents wear next their skin. "These are for you, one to wear and the other to bear. Down upon your knees, Mademoiselle Lisette; kiss this nice light rod and ask me to chastise you into a better and more fitting frame of mind. I shall only correct you with fatherly love."

Lisette kneels in considerable agitation, never having been subjected to punishment in her life. She kisses the rod—and for some moments is speechless with apprehension, till recollecting the other injunction of the Cure, she sobs out: "Oh! Oh! Father Dupris, have mercy! Pity me and forgive me; I will try and obey you in all things." Then, noticing his stern looks, "Oh! Oh! Not too severely if you must strike me," hiding her scarlet face in her hands.

The Cure is a man of rather advanced age and not very strong, his masculine vigour has long since been worn out by the great strain upon it in his younger days; but the sight of the tearful, shamefaced penitent at his feet sends quite a thrill of warmth through his usually chill veins.

Cure: "Stand up my daughter; you must wear this hair garment over your naked body; I must see you put it on, lace it up behind and seal the knot with wax, so you cannot take it off during your serious meditations; undress yourself quickly."

Lisette is too frightened and the Cure being an old man, she does not hesitate to obey, but is crimson at the shameful exposure, as she denudes herself one by one of the various articles of her clothing, till she stands quite naked before him, with nothing on but her pretty stockings and boots.

"Oh! Oh! Father Dupris, do make haste and let me dress again; I am so awfully ashamed to stand thus." She cries as he looks her all over and does not seem in any hurry with the hair garment.

Cure: "You are a figure to tempt St. Anthony himself; so much youthful grace and beauty ought to be consecrated to Heaven; it is sinful that such loveliness should ever be prostituted to the vile passions of mankind; you ought to take the veil, be the bride of Christ and a real daughter of the virgin; I will speak to your mother about it."

Lisette (in distress): "Oh! Oh! Father Dupris! Never! Never! I would rather die first, than be shut up in a convent."

Cure (angrily): "Your answer only shows the necessity of a severe penance," putting her arms through the sleeves of the hair garment and bringing it down over her beautiful bosom, he bungles and feels about the lovely globes, being scarcely able to refrain from kissing the delicate pink nipples, they look so inviting and impudent. "You'll find the roughness very irritating to your delicate skin, my daughter, but your penance must be severe; now turn your back to me while I lace it up tightly," which he does slowly, and then lighting a taper, selects a small seal from a drawer in the table and proceeds to drop the burning wax on the knot of the lace, purposely letting some of it fall on the bare flesh, where the garment cannot be quite drawn together. She screams with pain and to judge by his delighted looks, it gives him exquisite pleasure. "Poor thing, never mind Lisette, it was quite an accident," says he soothingly. "I would not hurt you unnecessarily for the world."

The hair vest comes just down half-way over her buttocks and leaves the plumpest part of her bottom and the pretty, soft, downy mount in front, uncovered. He pats her bottom lovingly and then with a hand-kerchief proceeds to blindfold her as, he assures her, "he does not wish her to see his distress as he has to flagellate her."

She patiently submits to it all and allows him to tie a cord round each of her wrists, little thinking what he is going to do, when he suddenly pulls them tight, and she finds herself almost hoisted off the ground, her toes just touching the floor whilst her arms are stretched wide apart, towards the hooks she had seen in the ceiling.

The old Cure (grinning with delight): "Now you wretched little sinner; your fat bottom shall smart before I let you down and I think I can make you promise to take the veil," beginning to switch her with the rod of twigs. "It's not too hard, I hope; you'll find it stings a little more presently."

Lisette: "Oh! Father Dupris spare me; let me down! Oh! how it smarts and cuts!" beginning to feel the first effects of his birching.

Cure: "Will you dismiss all love thoughts from your foolish noodle; or shall I draw them out of your tail?" His face is red and flushed as he enjoys all her contortions and cries for pity. He stops and wipes his spectacles in order to see clearly and not miss the slightest minutiae of her humiliation and distress.

It is an exquisite scene—that old man, birch in hand and spectacles on nose, gloating over his victim, as he stands with his legs wide apart and his left hand fumbling in his breeches with his poor old limp pego, which shows some incipient signs of a feeble rise; whilst the victim, Lisette, hangs by her distended arms, her fine plump bottom rendered more conspicuous by the tight-fitting hair vest and showing its rosy, blushing surface streaked with red lines where he has already treated it to a few light strokes.

The worn out old goat walks slowly round and even goes on his knees in front of her with his nose close to her fair, soft-looking cunny, to see as much as possible without actual touch.

Cure: "Poor Lisette; you little thought what a serious penance you would have to endure before I can eliminate all impurities from your mind; it distresses me beyond measure to have to whip you ever so lightly, but you must try to endure it and chasten your thoughts as I do mine daily; you saw the little scourge on the table; I use it on my own body every morning. How would you like to feel it? What do you think of that?" taking up the scourge and making two or three experimental strokes on the bursting skin of her bottom; the prickly pin points puncturing and drawing tiny drops of blood all over the surface.

Lisette: "Oh! Oh! Ah! Not that! Not that! Ah-r-r-re! it feels like a hundred small knives pricking me at once; Oh! Oh! I will put away all thoughts but my religious duties at such a solemn time as this," thinking to appease the Cure and get off.

Cure: "Your impudent-looking bottom must be well scored and made sore enough for you to remember this for a week or it will do you no good. I must now do my duty sternly or it will never be finished! I am so tender hearted," taking out his half-standing cock and frigging himself with the left hand as he cuts away again with his birch.

Lisette is in dreadful pain and plunges about in her distress so that her wrists are almost dislocated; each stroke makes her writhe her legs about, especially as the old fellow pays particular attention to her tender inner thighs, and now and then slyly lets the tips of the rod touch up the lips of her pussey.

He refrains from too heavy cuts; his pleasure is evidently to cause as much pain and smarting as possible without doing real damage, gradually wealing her bottom and thighs all over; his sharp cuts always laid on the tenderest parts. His excitement increases, and at last his affair looks quite manly in its vigorous stiffness. "Ah!" he exclaims, "if you could only see how distressed I am; it was quite right of me to blindfold you and spare you that suffering; oh! I pray the blessed virgin it may indeed do you good," cutting away with greater energy as he gets more excited and is beginning to lose his control on the rod.

Lisette (in agony): "My God! It's awful! Oh! Mercy! Mercy! Father Dupris, I shall die under it; my wrists are quite broken! Oh! Oh! what must I do to be spared? Ah-r-r-re!" giving a very prolonged shriek as he deals a tremendous whacker and sinks back exhausted into his chair.

Cure (recovering himself): "My exertions are too much for my age; will you promise now to devote yourself to Heaven and take the veil?" refreshing himself with a couple of glasses of wine and then picking up the light scourge says: "I can't use that heavy switch any more; this will bring you to repentance, Lisette."

Lisette, guessing what is going to happen, screams: "Oh! Pray don't use that other awful thing; it will bleed me to death; Oh! Oh! I will indeed do what you wish!"

Cure (laughing to himself in delight): "Ah! you say so now, but won't keep your promise. Will you swear to take the veil?" beginning to use the scourge, which draws a little blood at every cut and soon makes the punctured bottom crimson all over with blood stains.

Lisette (in great agony): "Oh! Oh! Yes! Let me down! Oh! Have mercy before I die! This is awful; I am going to faint!" which she does in reality before the old Cure can release her.

He lets her down and throws water over her face, but it is a long time before she regains consciousness and for some time before she comes to herself has a vague dreamy idea that some one is caressing and fondling her; she feels most lovingly excited and warm. In reality it is the old Cure who has not removed the bandage from her eyes for fear she might notice something when reviving. He has been inspecting and playing with her cunny; also kissing and licking her virgin charms.

Lisette (in a state of abstraction): "Ah! Oh! Where am I; I can't see!" putting her hand first on her mount, which she finds all wet and slimy, and then attempting to remove the bandage over her eyes. "Ah! I remember now, 'tis Father Dupris who has nearly killed me. How hot and sore my bottom is. How this nasty jacket pricks my skin, with its stiff hair!"

Cure: "Ah! My daughter; I have been praying by your side that this severe penance may indeed be your salvation from this wicked world; remember your promise; I will settle with your mother and arrange at the convent for your early reception."

Lisette is now thoroughly awake, but too frightened to remonstrate with Father Dupris who allows her to resume her clothing and finally dismisses her with a prayer and a blessing.

The poor girl returns to her mother and relates all that has occurred, beseeching with tears and entreaties to save her from the horrible convent, where she would be imprisoned and miserable for life. The mother is distressed, but too much under the influence of the Cure to dare to oppose him in the matter, as she consoles her poor child as well as possible, promising to intercede for her, but at the same time assuring her that Father Dupris is too good a man not to have her future welfare at heart. Lisette has to visit the Cure every day and receives several more penitential whippings from the lecherous old fellow, till at last she fairly consents to become a nun in the hopes of escaping any further persecution, but inwardly resolved to run away from the odious place if ever the opportunity should offer for a favourable attempt to regain her liberty.

Father Dupris evidently had some secret motive for thus compelling an unwilling but beautiful girl to sacrifice herself to religion, and as Lisette afterwards discovered, the Bishop and Abbot, with the chief monks of the Convent, which the nunnery formed only a part of, were the parties in the background, who urged their subordinate Cures and others to impress fresh victims from time to time, especially good looking girls.

Father Dupris escorted Madame Handelitte and

Lisette to the convent, where he introduced them to the Lady Superior, seeming especially to recommend the young lady to her favourable consideration.

They were most graciously received and assured that the nuns were indulged with every possible kindness and tended with a motherly love and solicitude for their earthly as well as spiritual welfare.

Lisette and her mamma had a painful leave-taking, which indeed proved their last, for they never met again, as when Madame Handelitte called to see her daughter a few days afterwards she was informed that she was seriously ill of typhus fever and afterwards that she was dead.

The poor lady was so affected by the news that she returned home and died in a few days of a broken heart, brought on by profound grief and remorse for having so parted with her daughter.

To return to Lisette. She was installed in a very cheerful cell, and being a novice, was not confined to such austere rules as those who had already taken the black veil. At the time of her entry into the convent she happened to be the only novice under probation, so that many of the nuns were continually conversing with her and talking of their happy, serene mode of life and exclusion from all the cares and sorrows of the outside world.

After two or three days a pretty dark eyed nun, called Sister Agnes, informed her that the Lady Superior had allotted herself to be a special companion to Lisette that they were to share a large cell between them, and study together all that was necessary to prepare her for the irrevocable vows she would have to take on assuming the black veil.

They occupied the same bed, and Sister Agnes soon won the heart of our novice, by her endearing ways, but affected no astonishment when she learnt the particulars of Lisette's treatment before admission to the convent saying:

"My dear, they served me as bad or worse before I came here. I feel myself so drawn towards you, that in confidence I will let you into all their secrets as far as is within my knowledge. I was as unwilling as ever you could have been to embrace conventual seclusion, but am now supposed to be quite resigned and contented, or I should never have been entrusted to be your companion. They would kill me outright if they only knew I ever told you of their doings, so I really place my life in your hands, dear Lisette; you don't know the awful wretches we have to do with!"

Lisette: (embracing Agnes with great affection) "We will indeed be sisters and faithful to each other; but tell me dear, did you really suffer more than I have?"

Agnes: "I am only seventeen now, and have been here two years, but never before found a confidante to whom I could unbosom myself. My father and mother both died about the same time, and being entitled to some considerable property, my uncles by connivance with the priest, shared my fortune, and forced me to take the veil; it was extorted from me just in the same manner as Father Dupris did with you; but in my case my eldest uncle who was my legal guardian, joined his Cure in torturing me; I was even suspended head downwards, and subjected to all sorts of indecencies and obscene treatment, besides being whipped to within an inch of my life till, like you, I promised anything to escape from them; but after all it was only out of the frying pan into the fire. This place is a very hell upon earth to a modest sensitive girl, till she gets inured to their brutality and filthiness.

"I confess it with shame but after a while I got even to feel pleasure, and gladly enter into their sensuality; it is the only enjoyment we are likely to be allowed in this place; besides I know that those who have resolutely refused ever to agree to their orgies, have been made away with, for fear they might some time find means to make it public and so create a scandal."

Lisette: "Oh! Horrible to think of; but I have been kindly treated, since I came here."

Agnes: "They won't let you alone long; you're too choice a morsel for them not to enjoy and humiliate you in every way; see and feel for yourself dear Lisette (they are in bed together) I have been ravished, both before and behind; it's awful at first, but afterwards gives most exquisite sensations and works one up to a blissful state of excitement. Let me feel you dear," putting her fingers into her virgin crack, and drawing Lisette closer to herself, till their naked bellies are in loving contact; in short during the first night, Sister Agnes managed to make Mademoiselle Lisette a most accomplished little tribade.

Two days after this, Sister Agnes, who had gone to early matins, on her return to their cell astonished Lisette by her flushed and excited appearance.

Lisette: "How hot you look; what is the matter, dear Agnes?"

Agnes: "The bishop has come on a visitation and this morning they have given an awful whipping before us all to a couple of plump good-looking nuns, who were caught cuddling each other in bed, as we do, dear Lisette (only no one can catch us in a cell by ourselves); they slept in a dormitory, where there are twenty beds, and one had got into bed with the other! they were surprised by the other occupants of the room who heard their suppressed sighs of pleasure and slyly struck a light; first they were dragged out of bed and their bottoms well slapped by all the nuns, till they almost fainted with the pain, and then reported to the Lady Superior, who reserved them for punishment by the Bishop and Abbot at visitation time. You are sure to be brought before them today or tomorrow; bear it all with fortitude, we shall have exquisite pleasure afterwards."

Lisette heard nothing of them that day, but at night Agnes reported that the reverend Father had been auditing the accounts of the nunnery; "and I believe my dear (between ourselves) inspecting the private charms of the Lady Superior and her favourite sisters, who no doubt, have quite monopolized them for the while; tomorrow they will want something more piquant and will send for you, and perhaps, I shall have to assist, or be a fellow victim; whatever I am compelled to do, rest assured dear Lisette, that it is only under compulsion, although I know I shall enter into the spirit of it, and enjoy most voluptuous sensations, as you will, by and bye, when you appreciate and understand it; but I think from some hints that have been dropped, they have got another victim girl with a big belly. She belongs to some great family, and is sent here to hide her shame." After passing a sleepless night of apprehension, poor Lisette was summoned early in the morning to attend the Bishop and members of the visitation court, who were assembled in the private apartment of the Lady Superior, she being seated at the right hand of the Bishop, with the Abbot of the monastery on his left, attended by three monks and three nuns respectively.

Lisette was accompanied by Sister Agnes, who led her into the room by the hand, and encouraged her as much as possible by cheerful advice, until the threshold was passed, and they stood in the solemn presence of the court, and were duly presented by the Lady Superior.

Lisette had just time to give a timid glance around the room, but could notice nothing but its sombre aspect, and that there were no hooks or pulleys attached to the ceiling, which was a little reassuring to her.

Bishop: (to Lady Superior) "Sister, is this the only novice you have at present to introduce to us?"

Lady Superior: "My Lord, I have another, but her's is a peculiar case of indiscretion. I thought you might prefer to see into it privately."

Bishop: "Let her be brought, nothing goes beyond these walls, and it may be a mutual benefit to each of them."

One of the nuns hastened from the apartment, and in a minute returned leading in a young girl of about eighteen, with a pale Grecian style of face, but with rich auburn hair and large expressive grey eyes, which scarcely dared to raise to the company, being in great confusion, her face paling and blushing by turns, evidently in shame at finding herself brought into the presence of several men.

Her figure showed signs of a very high stomach, as young ladies sometimes call it, and she appeared to be about six or seven months advanced in pregnancy.

Bishop: (in surprise) "Ha! by Heavens! 'tis the young lady De Tourville; her confessor had mentioned the sad case to me, but I little expected to meet her here," evidently highly pleased, and exchanging significant glances with the Abbot; "in the first place." he continued, "as these young persons are commencing their novicate they must be rechristened. Lisette Handelittle," looking at a slip of paper, handed him by the Lady Superior; "are you willing to take the veil!"

Lisette: "Oh! My Lord," falling on her knees, "take compassion on my case, my mother has no other child, and my promise was extorted from me by cruel whippings and penance."

Bishop: (frowning) "So you're a relapsed novice; this

must be seen to; such holy engagement cannot be lightly set aside; when you take the veil you will have the name of Elisabeth; Lisette is too frivolous for a convent, and must be altogether dropped."

The newly named Elizabeth rises to her feet, and after bowing to the Bishop, with eyes brimful of tears takes her place by the side of Sister Agnes, sighing and sobbing in hopeless distress.

Bishop: "Celine De Tourville your name is to be Magdalen, that you may always remember your fault; however high your birth, there is no distinction or difference here; all are Heavenly brides and sisters; are you a willing novice!"

Celine: (flushing scarlet) "Oh! My Lord, mine is indeed a shameful case; Seduced, I may say violated by my own father; I am now sent here for a life-long imprisonment to hide his disgrace and my own shame; I will never say I am a willing proselyte to your order of nuns."

The Bishop and Abbot have a short whispered consultation; then the former addressing the novices says, "We have determined to examine into your objections, in a few hours' time; meanwhile retire and reflect, as it would be far better for both of you to renounce all excuses, and embrace the Lady Superior as obedient and loving daughters."

About seven o'clock in the evening, when most of the nuns had already retired for the night, sisters Elizabeth and Agnes are again summoned, by the Lady Superior, and the Abbot; they have evidently been indulging in the pleasures of the table, for their faces are flushed, and their eyes sparkle with anticipated excitement. They, however, received the novices in a different apartment from that in which the morning sitting was held; it is more gloomy than the former, and in front of the Bishop is placed a couch covered with a hard looking pallet, and three round balls as bolsters, whilst close by stands a post, fixed in the floor, with iron rings arranged in it at various heights.

Bishop: "We will begin with sister Magdalen, as she seemed the more obstinate of the two this morning. What have you to say why we should not examine you, and inflict a proper penance, for your fornication and incest!"

Magdalen is silent and crimson with shame; she holds her hands clasped in front, with downcast eyes.

Bishop: "Sisters, do your duty; you understand me, we want no squalling babies in a nunnery, and I think the penance and punishment we shall impose, will prevent any living offspring of her incest ever coming to light."

Magdalen: (in terror as they begin to strip off her dress) "Oh! Oh! Will no one pity a poor ruined girl; the victim of her own father's lust; you, no doubt will absolve him; have mercy on me!" kneeling down and crying hysterically.

Bishop: "This is no time for tenderness; look at the voluptuous globes of her bosom, how they have grown; no doubt, her splendid development tempted a weak parent; she might have saved both him and herself by proper resistance."

Magdalen: (in deepest distress and humiliation) "Oh! Oh! you do not know what I suffered, before he succeeded in effecting my ruin."

Bishop: "All girls that commit fornication make some weak excuses; now make haste, remove her corset, and every rag;" evidently in a hurry to feast his eyes on her secret beauties, and conversing in an animated undertone with the Abbot and Lady Superior.

The nuns are most willing; they seem to enjoy the sight of Magdalen's shame and exposure, and their eyes sparkle with delight, as they pull off her chemise, leaving her quite naked for the Bishop and his coadjutors to inspect.

She has a beautiful figure, with a skin as white as snow, large full bosom, with lovely pink nipples, wide spreading hips, and splendid buttocks, as hard and firm as ivory; her belly is beautifully bowed out, and adorned below by short, curly, light red hair, on a luscious looking mount, whilst her pregnant state makes her cunny very conspicuous, and especially the red pouting lips, as they place her on the couch, putting a bolster under her bottom, and open her legs wide to give the old Bishop a good view. They all get up, and crowd round her, and the Bishop who evidently is his own M.C., stoops over her cunny, poking his fingers in, nipping her clitoris and the pouting lips explaining especially to the Lady Superior all the symptoms of pregnancy which the Lady also evidently enjoys, without a blush whilst their poor victim cries and screams for them not to degrade her so shamefully. This lasts for some minutes, the Abbot and monks also assisting in handling the poor girl all over, paying particular attention to her bottom and bosom.

Bishop: "Now, we will proceed to examine her, tie her up to the post; we must have all the revolting particulars of this incestuous intercourse from her, in order that the father may be properly dealt with by the Church. Brother Paul will take it all down in writing as she is compelled to tell us."

Magdalen is secured to the post in a most painful manner, both her ankles and wrists being fastened to rings, quite close to the floor, so that notwithstanding her big belly, she is almost bent double.

Bishop: "That's it, the skin of her bottom is finely stretched, give me a scourge with steel tips," going on his knees behind Magdalen so as to get a delightful view of pussey and bottom together.

He takes the scourge from one of the monks, and begins to apply it briskly to the bent rump, every stroke pricking and puncturing the skin, so that the blood oozes in profusion all over the surface, making her scream piteously for mercy.

Bishop: "You want mercy, Magdalen, do you? Then you must tell us all about it; how did your father first commence with you?"

Magdalen: "He took me on his knee one day, before I was quite fifteen, and kissing me, put his hand up my clothes threw me into great confusion and distress, putting his finger up my bottom, and working it there for a long time, making me quite hot and wet; then he handled me in front, rubbing two of his fingers in my slit, till I could not help wetting them all over, with a kind of greasy thick fluid, that gushed from me all of a sudden, at which he laughed and seemed delighted, especially at my shamefaced blushes, which he kissed away, and assured me he had a right to amuse himself with his daughter."

Bishop: (who had been listening with great pleasure) "Was that all? he did not make that big belly so; go on if you want to save yourself from my scourge;" giving her a couple of reminders.

Magdalen: "Ah! Oh! Have mercy, be patient and I will confess all I can tell, and keep nothing back.

"Another day, he opened his trousers and showed me what he had; a hard stiff thing, growing out of a bed of air at the bottom of his belly; he made me handle and play with it till it suddenly spouted a lot of nasty stuff in my face, at which he laughed, and told me nothing could be wrong that my father did or thought right; this sort of thing continued for some time, till one day in spite of my cries and distress, he forced the big thing right up my bottom, and discharged there, which he often did afterwards, till one day he said he could not help himself and must have my virginity. I begged and implored him with tears to spare me, and consider the consequences, but he threw me on a couch, forced himself between my legs, and never desisted till after excruciating rending, and thrusting through the delicate parts, he had thoroughly ravished me. Now you know all. Oh! Oh! Have mercy! My Lord!"

Bishop: "That did not make you enceinte, you must have been libidinous, and enjoyed it with him or it could never have happened; you wanton girl;" touching her up once more.

Magdalen: "Ah! Oh! How could I help myself? He did it so often that at last I did feel pleasure, and responded to his action; Ah indeed how could I help myself? Oh! Father, cruel Father! What misery have you brought to me!" And she is almost ready to faint with shame and the painful effects of their treatment.

Bishop: "You must remain as you are for the present till Sister Elizabeth is also ready, then we will finish your punishment!"

Agnes and the nuns at a sign from the Lady Superior, quickly proceed to disrobe Elizabeth and in a minute or two, her chemise is pulled off and her modesty is only protected by her drawers, as she keeps her legs tightly nipped together.

Bishop: (angrily) "How's this, no one ought to wear such things in a convent, drawers are most unseemly, the hair vest is removed but she prevents you removing her trousers, does she! Ha! I have an idea, mount her up on Magdalen's back, and the Lady Superior shall operate with a good birch upon the obstinate bottom; she knows how to cut such things off, I warrant."

Agnes' eyes glisten with excitement and her colour

heightens, with the anticipation of pleasure to come; but poor Elizabeth is terribly afraid and ashamed, as they hoist her up, and set her astride of Magdalen's loins, and fasten her hands to the rings in the post; the enceinte girl groans at the imposition of such a heavy burden in her constrained and cramped position; but their persecutors have no bowels of compassion; every fresh torture only serves as stimulant to further acts of cruelty.

Lady Superior, who has been furnished with a fine heavy bunch of birch, now advances to the front; she is a fine dark woman, about five and thirty, with raven hair and black piercing eyes, now all aglow with animation; she has no veil on, and with one hand gathers the skirts of her robe, showing a fine pair of legs in flesh coloured silken hose, and pretty lavender kid shoes, which she evidently assumed for the special occasion; the right hand grasps the rod, and she looks the picture of offended dignity, about to avenge itself upon a rebellious girl's rump, as she orders them to open the drawers behind and pin them back, then says, "the girl knows I told her no such things were allowed here; how dare you, Elizabeth, come into the presence of his Lordship with such improper things on?"

Elizabeth: "Oh! Oh! Lady Mother! Forgive me, I never expected to be so shamefully exposed."

Lady Superior: "My Lord! I have no patience, the girl is obstinate in every respect; I must begin; if I am carried away by my zeal for her future good, I trust to your wisdom to check my ardour. Now then—one—two—three:" giving a good sounding blow to commence with, and increasing the force at every cut "four—five—six;" each whack making the poor girl's bottom fairly spring under the concussion, as if she was in reality riding a horse. The white skin is scarlet all over, and marked with deep red lines, where the blood is drawn up in weals.

Elizabeth: "Oh! Oh! How cruel; Have Mercy; Oh! What must I do?" Plunging about in great agony, almost making Magdalen fall under her.

Magdalen: "Oh! Oh! I can't bear her; she kicks so; I shall be injured! Oh! Take her off me!"

Lady Superior: "You may both scream; it will do you good; there Magdalen, there Elizabeth;" she keeps repeating; "I must whip you both;" cutting them alternately with great force, till both bottoms are well scored and bleeding.

The Bishop and spectators are all greatly excited; he gets hold of Agnes, lays her across his knee, and turning up her clothes, is assisted by the Abbot in spanking her bottom tremendously, with their open hands. The three monks each take one of the nuns and serve her the same, making them shriek with pain, and kick and writhe under the smarting smacks.

This goes on for several minutes, and Elizabeth, hearing so many cries, turns her head, but has only just time to comprehend the scene before the Lady Superior cuts her across the face, exclaiming, "How dare you turn round;" and is about to repeat the blow, when Elizabeth feels poor Magdalen give way under her, and falls to the floor, hanging by her hands to the post; this seems to infuriate the Lady Superior more than ever, and she cuts both of them all over their bodies and faces; never heeding that Magdalen has really fainted; taking especial delight in cutting and wealing that poor girl's distended belly, till at last the Bishop looking up for a moment from his amusement, exclaims: "Good God! Brother, that woman will murder the girl outright; she is quite beside herself; pull her away, you know how to soothe her, and bring her around;" laughing "Ha! Ha! Ha! Sister Agnes, your bottom is a rosebud, jump up and help me with the victims;" giving a tremendous slap, which makes the girl fairly gasp for breath as she suddenly rises and goes to the post; calling out. "Look sharp, Agnes, we must blindfold them."

The victims have bandages put over their eyes, and then Elizabeth knows no more about poor Magdalen but feels herself lifted up and placed on the couch, face upward, with a pillow under her bottom, a hard, hot, fleshy substance is poked into her slit, some person holds her legs wide open, and she feels another one standing between them, pushing himself closer and closer, gradually forcing his instrument into her vagina by vigorous painful thrusts. She screams, "Ah! Ah! Oh! Ah-r-r-re!" as it splits and rends through her hymen, deluging her with a warm injection of soothing sperm, which greatly eases her, and alleviates the pain of the ravishment, causing her heated and excited parts to slightly respond to the motions within her, and presently, when the man has withdrawn, she lies still, in a listless, lethargic state of semi-consciousness.

She is not allowed to remain quiet long, but presently finds herself laid on her belly, with the pillow under her loins, and her bottom well elevated on the edge of the couch, with her feet just touching the floor; some one parts the cheeks of her bottom, and shoves a finger roughly into the little orifice causing her great pain and making her scream again and again. "Oh! Oh! Oh! Ah! It is shameful! you hurt me so! Oh! I will do anything, if you have mercy and spare me!"

Bishop: "She is getting more docile, we shall make a proper novice of her presently; she will be more useful to us even than Agnes when we have properly christened her bottom."

Just at this moment the bandage slips almost off

Elizabeth's eyes, and she catches a glimpse of poor Magdalen covered with blood, and apparently lifeless, being borne from the apartment by two of the monks, who to judge from their sanguineous appearance have frightfully abused her. She also sees the old Bishop with nothing on but his shirt, with his rampant cock in one hand whilst the Lady Superior, in her chemise, is sitting on his knee kissing him most lasciviously; it is the Abbot who is ramming his rough finger up into her fundus so painfully, and Agnes is applying a scourge of small cords to his exposed posteriors, looking a veritable young harlot in her almost nude and dishevelled state; her eyes and face beaming with voluptuous excitement, although to judge from the red stains on her chemise, she must have been cruelly whipped and ill treated herself.

Abbot: "Don't let her see, throw something over her head."

This is soon done; one of the nuns throws her habit over poor Elizabeth's head, and all her further experience is confined to the senses of feeling and hearing.

Abbot: "Give me that scourge, my backside has been so used to that plaything for years; you are doing no good, girl; there now, see how I will garnish her bottom-hole for her; you just kneel in front and play with my pego, till I am quite ready to enculer."

Elizabeth hears all this, and the next moment she shrieks in agony, at the tremendous stroke which crashes on her bum, and seems to cut the skin quite through; the blows continue to fall rapidly, especially close to her fundus; she hears the heavy breathing of the old fellow, as he gets blown with his exertions, but it is quite regardless of her agonizing cries; her bottom streams with blood, and she feels as if pieces of flesh were being cut out of her rump with red hot knives.

Elizabeth: "Oh! Oh! Ah-r-r-re! My God! How awful! Oh! It would be a great mercy to kill me outright! Oh! Ah-r-r-re!" she shrieks, and feels no more, having gone off in a swoon.

She does not know how long she remained so, but presently awoke with an awful pain in her bottom-hole, which is being rent and forced in by his big cock, which she feels already quite a couple of inches inside her fundus. Her renewed cries only elicit shouts of delight and laughter, till at last the old monster fairly screams:

"Oh! Oh! I must come now; how delightful! Oh! Agnes hold my testicles tight!" As he gets completely in, and spends a profusion of soothing juice into her bowels. She faints again and only awakes to find Agnes bathing and washing the injured parts, as she lies on her bed in her own cell.

It would take too long to tell you all the further tortures poor Elizabeth underwent, during several months. The wretched Magdalen died in childbed, being unable to give birth to her dead child, under the unskillful treatment of the nuns. Elizabeth and Agnes both escaped from the Convent and came to Paris, as I told you before; but the latter soon got married by a sympathising Protestant, whilst Lisette resumed her old name, and became a fatuous member of the demi-monde.

Sir Charles: "The story is most interesting; is Lisette still in Paris?"

Count: "Oh, yes! she is still young and beautiful."

Sir Charles: "We have drawn out the evening, but I must have one more scene before we part; what do you say to a bouquet of victims?"

Madame: "We can arrange four round the ladder, Haidee, Flora, Veneria and Melissa; whilst you two gentlemen shall have a victim each; Sophie for

Charles, and Alice for the Count, placed face downward on the table, myself and Lucidora with good birches will walk round and round, and keep the four well alive."

Sir Charles: "A birch is not good enough for me; we must have cats; what say you, Count?"

Count: "Yes, yes, Sir Charles, we want something more effective, to rouse us for a final effort."

The arrangements are soon complete, Sophia and Alice are laid across the table, and their bottoms well opened by tying the right ankle of one victim to the left ankle of the other, whilst the remaining two feet are also secured to the legs of the table; their hands are also well fastened under the table so that they are quite helpless, with their posteriors most favourably projected to meet any kind of attack. The gentlemen commence softly with their cats and gradually increase the force of their blows as they warm to their work, till the blood begins to flow freely; this excites their fury; they are deaf to the pitiful heart-rending cries of Alice and Sophia who scream fearfully and are soon terribly cut up. It is a maddening scene, both gentlemen and all the victims are quite naked; Madame and Lucidora in demi-toilette, with flashing eyes and flushed faces, apply their birches rapidly to the bottoms of the four girls secured to the ladder, making them keep up quite a chorus of screams and writhe and caper in every possible variety of exciting contortions. Sir Charles and his friend are soon quite beside themselves, but cut on till their victims are a mass of bruised and bleeding wounds, from their backs all down their thighs, and in between the tenderest place; till seeing them nearly ready to swoon, they throw aside their cats, and with the assistance of Madame and Lucidora, soon find themselves in full possession of the tight bottom holes of Sophia and Alice. The Count manages to enculer and make Alice quite forget all her sufferings by his lively and stimulating movements; but Sir Charles has a frightful effort to make before he gets fairly into Sophie's virgin orifice. The poor girl screams awfully and faints outright with the pain, whilst to stimulate Sir Charles they bring little Melissa and make her observe what he is doing to her sister, asking her "how she would like it herself, etc.," to the infinite terror and shame of the poor little thing and the great delight of the gentlemen, who order all the disengaged girls to kneel and play with their testicles and bottom frig them and stimulate them in every possible way to a renewed enculade which the throbbing and delightful pressures of the invaded sphincters soon bring about again; and they have a second glorious spend before withdrawing.

This is the closing of the séance and they all retire to their respective apartments.

Next day Haidee and Flora have a consultation with Sir Charles and the Count; the two young ladies are now completely converted and anxious to assist in any way to further the future voluptuous amusements of the gentlemen and agree to accompany Madame to Paris to engage in their séances and also to look after a few orphan girls for fresh victims.

THE END.

BIRCHGROVE PRESS

Flagellant & Libertine Erotica

Birchgrove Press specializes in producing new print and e-book editions of pre-1950s writings on sexual flagellation in English. Original editions of many of the books that we offer are difficult to obtain and are highly sought after. We are especially proud to offer new editions of rare Victorian flagellant texts such as *The Mysteries of Verbena House*, *Experimental Lecture by Colonel Spanker*, and *The Quintessence of Birch Discipline*. Birchgrove Press also produces new editions of libertine literature. We have published *Venus in the Cloister*, *The School of Venus*, *The Dialogues of Luisa Sigea*, and Isidore Liseux's translation of the Marquis de Sade's *Justine* (1791), *Opus Sadicum*, for example. For a full list of titles and formats, please visit our website:

www.birchgrovepress.com.

www.ingramcontent.com/pod-product-compliance
Lightning Source LLC
Chambersburg PA
CBHW071248130626
46556CB00003B/1216